W9-AAS-639

Mermaid KINGDOM

Deep-Water Drama

by Janet Gurtler
illustrated by Katie Wood

CAPSTONE YOUNG READERS
a capstone imprint

Mermaid Kingdom is published by
Capstone Young Readers
A Capstone Imprint
1710 Roe Crest Drive
North Mankato, Minnesota 56003
www.mycapstone.com

Copyright © 2016 Capstone Young Readers

Library of Congress Cataloging-in-Publication Data

Names: Gurtler, Janet, author. | Wood, Katie, 1981- illustrator. | Gurtler, Janet. Mermaid kingdom.
Title: Deep-water drama / by Janet Gurtler ; illustrated by Katie Wood.
Description: North Mankato, Minnesota : Capstone Young Readers, a Capstone imprint, [2016] | Series: Mermaid kingdom | Summary: In this compilation of three separately published works, Shyanna, Rachel, and Cora, three thirteen-year-old mermaids in the Kingdom of Neptunia, have their friendships tested by secrets, worries, and other challenges.
Identifiers: LCCN 2015032920 | ISBN 978-1-62370-632-6 (paper over board)
Subjects: LCSH: Mermaids--Juvenile fiction. | Best friends--Juvenile fiction. | Friendship--Juvenile fiction. | Secrecy--Juvenile fiction. | Trust--Juvenile fiction. | CYAC: Mermaids--Fiction. | Best friends--Fiction. | Friendship--Fiction. | Secrets--Fiction. | Trust--Fiction.
Classification: LCC PZ7.G9818 De 2016 | DDC 813.6--dc23
LC record available at http://lccn.loc.gov/2015032920

Designer: Alison Thiele

Artistic Elements: Shutterstock

Printed and bound in the USA.

009746R

Mermaid Life

Mermaid Kingdom refers to all the kingdoms in the sea, including Neptunia, Caspian, Hercules, Titania, and Nessland. Each kingdom has a king and queen who live in a castle. Merpeople live in caves.

Mermaids get their legs on their thirteenth birthdays at the stroke of midnight. It's a celebration when the mermaid makes her first voyage onto land. After their thirteenth birthdays, mermaids can go on land for short periods of time but must be very careful.

If a mermaid goes on land before her thirteenth birthday, she will get her legs early and never get her tail back. She will lose all memories of being a mermaid and will be human forever.

Mermaids are able to stay on land with legs for no more than forty-eight hours. Any longer and they will not be able to get their tails back and will be human forever. They will lose all memories of being a mermaid.

If they fall in love, merpeople and humans can marry and have babies (with special permission from the king and queen of their kingdom). Their babies are half-human and half-merperson. However, this love must be the strongest love possible in order for it to be approved by the king and queen.

Half-human mermaids are able to go on land indefinitely and can change back to a mermaid anytime. However, they are not allowed to tell other humans about the mermaid world unless they have special permission from the king and queen.

Part One: Shyanna's Tale

Chapter One

It was almost the big day! Only one more night until my birthday! Everyone loves to have a birthday, but this year was extra special because I was going to turn thirteen. In Mermaid Kingdom, turning thirteen is a VBD (very big deal). At midnight on thirteenth birthdays, merpeople go to land and get to use legs for the first time. After that, our legs can be used on land for a few hours at a time. I was so excited to be able to join my best friends, Rachel and Cora, for adventures on land.

I loved being a mermaid and I loved the ocean, but there was something about breathing air and having legs that intrigued me, too.

"Shyanna!" my mom called while I braided my hair and imagined myself skipping on the beach.

"What's up, Mom?" I shouted from my room as I finished up my hair. I imagined she was curious about which song I'd selected to sing at my midnight leg ceremony. The leg ceremony was totally magical.

"Have you finished with the shell decorations you and the girls were working on for the Neptunia Day parade?" my mom called.

I rolled my eyes at the reflection in my mirror. The mirror was a treasure my dad had found in an old shipwreck. He'd given it to me right before he disappeared two years earlier.

Neptunia may have been the best kingdom in the ocean, but there were always dangers underwater. From humans and nets to sharks and storms, the ocean was a dangerous place to live. Anything could happen at any time, and nobody really knows what happened to my dad. Although it's getting easier, my mom and I still miss him every day.

"They're done," I called. "We left them on the kitchen table."

"Thank goodness. We have to finish up all the details for the Queen's float this morning. You girls are lifesavers!" she called. "I was up so late last night going over all the last-minute details with the parade committee. I never could have done them on my own." She swam into my room and smiled at me. "You look so beautiful. I can't believe it's your last day as a twelve-year-old mergirl!"

Mom was always super busy for Neptunia Day because she was the leader of the parade committee. Unfortunately, this year Neptunia Day fell on the same day as my birthday. It was kind of overshadowing my big day, but I was trying hard not to let it ruin things.

We looked at each other in my mirror, and then she sighed. "I wish I didn't have to be so busy with the parade committee today. But I have to finish up all the float preparations. The Queen likes things to be perfect. Speaking of perfect, we'll make all the final arrangements for your leg ceremony tonight. Okay? You must be so excited!"

"I really am, " I said. "I can't wait to have legs so I can go with Rachel and Cora to see Owen on land and meet his friends!"

Owen was Rachel's best friend and a human. Because Rachel was half-human and half-mermaid, she could go on land whenever she wanted for as long as she wanted. That's how she met Owen. Rachel often felt weird because she was both human and mermaid, but I thought it was amazing. I was a little jealous.

"Well, you won't see Owen and any of his friends at your leg ceremony," she said. "It's too late at night, and Owen and his friends will be sleeping."

"I know that," I told her. "I meant later. When I go to land with Cora and Rachel. Also, I decided on a small leg ceremony. Just Rachel and Cora and their families."

"Sounds good," she said, but I could tell she was losing focus.

"I'm so excited you're going on land with me. I know it's been a long time for you," I continued, hoping to spend a little more time with my mom before she had to leave again.

"Mm hmm. Good." She nodded as she checked through the shell purse slung over her shoulder. "So what are you doing today?"

"I'm meeting Cora and Rachel at Walrus Waterpark to hang out and go over my plans. We might go swim with dolphins later or take Cora's sisters to watch sea turtles."

"Oh darn," my mom said, clearly not even listening. "I forgot the list with the order of the parade floats." She swam closer and kissed my forehead again. "I have to find it before I go. Sorry I'm so wrapped up in Neptunia Day," she added.

"It's okay," I said, even though I wished my birthday didn't coincide with Neptunia Day. It was a great day of celebration for our castle, with a big parade and lots of other fun events. It went on all day and late into the night. And I didn't want to seem selfish, but it seemed like with the preparations and timing, everyone was forgetting about my birthday. Thirteen was a huge deal, and getting my legs for the first time was an even bigger deal.

"I have to run," Mom said. "I'm so sorry, but we'll talk about everything you've planned at our spa appointment tomorrow. Meanwhile, I'm so glad Rachel and Cora are around to help you with your plans. You're so lucky to have them. Such great best friends." She wiped away a smear of algae on my mirror and frowned. "It's been such a long time since I've been on land." Her lips turned down more, and she sighed.

"I'll see you later. Have a good day," she said absently as she swam off to fetch the decorations.

My mom seemed more distracted than usual, which didn't make me feel confident that my birthday plans would work out. The leg ceremony was a big deal, and without my mom I couldn't do it. Her distraction made me feel nervous — very, very nervous.

Chapter Two

"Hey, almost-birthday girl!" Cora said when I swam into Walrus Waterpark. As always, Cora's baby sister was tucked under her arm and another sister swam in front of her, giggling as she tried to get away.

"I can't believe my mom volunteered to work with yours on the parade committee this year," Cora said. "Now I'm stuck looking after my sisters all day long." She sighed dramatically as she put Jewel into the baby swing and then pushed her other two sisters.

For once I agreed with her. I loved Cora's sisters despite all their shenanigans, but they were a lot of work. I always wished I had sisters of my own, but today I kind of wanted things to be about my plans.

"Can you take them with us to swim with the dolphins later?" I asked, kind of knowing the answer already. I swam over and took over Jewel's swing.

"No. They're too young. We'll have to do it another time," Cora said.

I nodded, trying not to show my disappointment. "I wonder where Rachel is," I said, looking around the park. "She's not usually late."

"She's been working on a new number for the Spirit Squad," Cora said. "She probably lost track of time."

Rachel was kind of obsessed with coming up with new routines for the group to perform. We were all on the squad, but Rachel was the most involved.

"Oh," I said, trying not to show the resentment that was creeping around my insides. I was bummed that no one seemed to be very concerned about my birthday or seemed to want to help with my plans. I'd been looking forward to it for as long as I could remember. Turning thirteen and having your leg ceremony was so important, and nobody seemed to care. Not my mom, and not my best friends.

“What are you wearing to the parade?” Cora asked as she pushed one sister in the swing and swam over quickly to push the other's beside her.

I sighed, sick of Neptunia Day and all its birthday attention robbing. I wanted to talk about what I should wear to my leg ceremony, not the stupid parade. I wanted to talk about how I should do my hair and what color I should paint my nails. I was so over the parade, and it hadn't even started yet.

“I don't know,” I told Cora, rolling my eyes just a little. “My mom and I are going to the spa before the parade, and I hadn't really thought about it too much. I'm more concerned about what I'm going to wear that night.”

I was just about to tell Cora what happened with my mom and how I was feeling about my leg ceremony when Rachel swam into the park.

"Sorry I'm late!" she cried before I could mutter any more complaints about my birthday plans. Rachel swam to the swings and did a flip in front of the sisters to make them laugh. Her long red hair flowed out behind her. I wished I could get my hair to curl and spring freely like hers. It would be the perfect style for my leg ceremony.

"I was at Cassie's cave," Rachel said. Cassie was the songwriter for the Spirit Squad, and she and Rachel spent lots of time working together.

I was happy Rachel was making new friends. She'd had a hard time with some of the merkids when she and her dad moved to Neptunia. Most of us thought it was cool she was half-human and could use her legs on land whenever she wanted to. But some merkids hadn't been so nice about it, and Rachel had some trust issues.

I was glad Rachel loved the Spirit Squad and had made new friends, but was it wrong that I kind of wanted some of her attention on me now?

Rachel and Cora both played with me for a while, but they were both really distracted. Before long they both left, and my birthday had hardly even been mentioned.

Chapter Three

That night Mom got home late again. She was exhausted from all her hard work with the parade committee. We ate leftovers and decided to talk about my birthday plans in the morning because she was too tired. So much for getting everything in order for my birthday. I felt like nobody had time for me, and it was really starting to make me sad.

Mom wanted to go to bed early, so I pretended I was tired too and ended up sadly staring at the ceiling until late in the night.

When I opened my eyes in the morning, I stretched my arms and smiled. It was my birthday! I was thirteen! I would finally get my legs!

I swam out of bed. “Mom?” I called.

No one answered. The cave was quiet.

I swam from my room. I swam into the kitchen. There was a note on the table next to a bowl and my favorite kind of cereal.

“Happy Birthday, Shyanna! I had to go check out a problem with the Queen’s float. I’ll be back as soon as I can. Be ready to go to the spa when I get home!”

Things were too silent and unfestive. This was not how I wanted my birthday to start. I tried not to be disappointed and softly hummed the “Happy Birthday” song to myself as I ate. I tried to enjoy the peace and quiet.

After breakfast, I swam to the front yard. It was even quiet out there. The only things I saw were some small snails playing a slow and noiseless game of hide-and-seek. I guessed that everyone was too

Happy birthday, Shyanna!
I had to go check out a problem with the Queen's float.
I'll be back as soon as I can.
Be ready to go to the spa when I get home!
xx

busy getting things in order for Neptunia Day to care about my birthday.

I felt eyes on me and looked around hopefully, but it was only a scallop watching me. He was bright and beautiful with his fan-shaped shell, so I waved hello. I hoped he'd come over and offer some company, but he ignored my gesture and swam away, opening and closing his shell to move. I have never felt so lonely in my life!

I sighed, but then I heard the phone ringing from inside our cave. It had to be Rachel or Cora, and they'd probably burst into the birthday song as soon as I picked it up. I hurried inside and grabbed the phone with a big smile on my face.

"Hello?" I sang.

"Shyanna?" It was my mom. And I could tell she wasn't happy just by the way she said my name.

"Hi, Mom," I said. "Are you okay?

"I'm fine, Shy. Things have just gotten crazy around here. We have a bit of an emergency. A hammerhead shark smashed up the Queen's float. We're working really hard to get it fixed, but I don't know how long I'm going to be delayed. I'm trying to get away, but there's no one else to handle things. Do you think . . . would you mind terribly if one of the girls went to the spa in my place? I feel so badly, but I have no idea how long I'll take, and I don't want you to miss your appointment because of me."

My heart sank to the ocean floor. "Of course not, Mom. Don't worry about it. I'll ask Rachel or Cora to come. It'll be fine. Fun!"

I didn't mention that we were supposed to finalize my plans for the leg ceremony. I still had to choose my song, and we hadn't figured out what Mom was going to wear to coordinate with my outfit for our walk on land together.

"Cora's mom is with me," Mom went on, "so Cora's probably busy watching her sisters. I'm sure Rachel will love it, though! Have fun. I'll be home as soon as I can!" Then she hung up the phone.

A tear slid out of my eye as I put the phone down. She hadn't even said goodbye.

I called Rachel, but her dad answered. "Sorry, Shyanna," he said. "Rachel went to land to see Owen. He has some new songs to teach her, and she wanted to incorporate them into the new Spirit Squad routine. She sure loves that group. But hey, happy birthday! Today's the big day! Can't wait to see you on your new legs tonight!"

"Thanks, Mr. Marlin," I said, thankful that at least someone was around to wish me a happy birthday. I seriously considered asking him to go to the spa with me, but decided that would be way too awkward for both of us.

I sighed when I hung up the phone, feeling like the biggest loser in Mermaid Kingdom. It was my birthday, and I was all alone! My birthday was a complete disaster.

I knew I could ask another mergirl to go with me to the spa. I had plenty of friends from school, and anyone would be happy to have a free spa date. But it didn't feel right to ask just anyone. And besides, no one else had been invited to my leg ceremony. It seemed selfish and last minute to ask someone else to join me to celebrate now.

I'd go alone. How bad could it be?

Chapter Four

"You'll start your song quietly as you emerge from the water at exactly midnight," Star Fishery, the beautician at the spa explained as she painted my fingernails.

Star had been thrilled when she found out it was my birthday. She actually shouted loudly with joy when I told her I was thirteen. When she heard about my mom's emergency, she immediately started helping me plan my leg ceremony. She even helped me decide on my song and insisted I practice singing.

Despite my stage fright and all the other mermaids in the spa, I managed to sing the whole thing out loud. Everyone clapped when I was done and assured me I would have the most perfect leg ceremony ever.

"When you get your legs, you start to build up the song at a louder crescendo. The moon is full tonight, so you'll be lit by soft glowing light," Star said. "We'll undo your braids so your hair will flow all curly and bouncy around your pretty face." She giggled with delight, and her enthusiasm was infectious and warmed my woeful heart. "It will be magical — completely magical and unforgettable. The way every leg ceremony is meant to be."

"Do you really think so?" I asked, starting to feel a lot better about my special day. Leave it to Star to bring the magic back.

"I do," she said. "I know you wish your mama was here, but I'm going to help you and make you so beautiful it will be a night you'll never forget.

What color is your outfit? I'll apply matching starfish decals on your nails!"

I told her what I planned to wear: the purple shell top and matching necklaces. She nodded with enthusiasm. She rubbed my tail with sparkly oil and added rainbow glitter to my hair. She said the hair glitter would last all day and shimmer in the light of the full moon. The excitement in the spa helped me get in the mood for the day, and my sadness about being forgotten disappeared.

As I got up from the chair, everyone cheered and whistled. Then Star started off a round of "Happy Birthday" and everyone sang. I floated out of the shop and swam back toward my cave, finally feeling special and happy.

With all the extra work Star put in at the spa, I was home a little later than expected. I swam in the front door of the cave, excited to show my mom how incredible I looked.

"Mom!" I sang when I swam into our cave, already holding out my hand so she could admire my birthday nails up close. I wasn't going to dwell on the fact that it was the mermaid at the spa who helped me plan the final details for my leg ceremony. Nothing could take away from my big day now! Everything was set and it was going to be perfect.

"Mom?" I shouted again.

There was no answer. In fact, our cave was eerily quiet.

I swam into the kitchen. "Mom?" I said, but no one said a word. I swam around the cave and realized, with heart-crushing certainty, that she wasn't home.

There was no clam cake. There were no sea balloons or presents on the table. The Neptunia Day parade was more important to her than I was. All of my excitement from the spa evaporated in one big sigh.

I didn't want to cry, but I could barely hold back the tears anymore.

I grabbed the phone and called Rachel's cave. Maybe her dad knew where my mom was. No one at the Marlin residence answered. I frowned and then dialed Cora's number. No one picked up there, either. Were they all out enjoying the Neptunia Day festivities without me? Had they completely forgotten about my birthday? I glanced at the clock as I put the phone back on the table.

It was already past dinnertime, and I hadn't heard from my two best friends or my mom in hours. I swam slowly to my room, catching a reflection of my shimmering tail in my special mirror on the cave wall.

If my dad was here, would I be all alone on my thirteenth birthday? I swam inside my room, my heart heavy and tears bubbling up in the corners of my eyes.

"Shyanna!" a voice shouted from outside the cave.

I frowned. Was that Rachel's voice? It sounded panicked.

I swam toward my door as Rachel burst inside.

"Rachel!" I cried. Finally, someone had come to see me on my birthday! But then I saw her face. It was pale and worried. She didn't look happy or excited. She looked terrified. What was going on?

"Thank goodness you're here!" she said.

I frowned, but before I could ask what was wrong, she grabbed my hand and pulled me.

"Come on. We have to go. Fast! Jewel is trapped in a fishing net!" she shouted. "We're too big to get her out. We need you. You're her last hope."

Chapter Five

My heart pounded like waves crashing onto shore as Rachel and I swam up through the water to the fishing net where Jewel was stuck.

"Cora and I tried to get her out, but we're too big," Rachel explained as we swam faster than I thought I could swim. "You are the only one small enough to help her. Your mom is there, and my dad and Cora's family, but no one can get to her."

"What was everyone doing when she got stuck?" I asked.

She glanced at me. "I'll explain later."

We swam so quickly that everything was a blur, and in a few minutes we reached the net. My tail ached, and the shine and shimmer from the spa had completely disappeared from kicking so hard, but none of that mattered when I saw Jewel.

Baby Jewel was inside a net, trapped and squished up against hundreds of fish of various sizes. Her whole family and my mom and Rachel's dad were gathered outside of the net, following it with terrified helpless looks on their faces as it dragged along the ocean floor. It was eerily quiet as the net moved, like it was all a bad dream. All the nearby sea creatures were hiding, frightened.

Cora was at my side in an instant when she saw me. "Oh, Shyanna!" she cried. "We've tried and tried, but we're too big to slip into the net. Jewel can't make her way out alone. She doesn't understand how, and she's too worked up to listen to us. She needs someone to go in and get her."

"I'll go," I said without hesitation. Being small for my age was finally a benefit for once. On top of being small, I was really flexible. It was my time to step up and help.

"Be careful, Shyanna," my mom said, patting my shoulder as I swam by.

Cora's mom had three little mergirls clinging to her, and Cora's dad had his arm around her. "Please help," he whispered. I nodded and swam past. There was no time to talk. Rachel and Cora swam with me to the net.

"If you can slip inside the hole, you can help get Jewel out," Cora said. Her voice was strained and nervous. "You have to get her out!"

I nodded and swam to the net, grabbing at the thick scratchy rope. It pulled away from my hands as if it sensed what I was about to do, almost taking my fingernails right off.

"Oh!" I shouted, surprised. When I pulled my hand back, I caught a glimpse of my nails. My new manicure was destroyed, but I knew that didn't matter. The only thing that mattered right now was Jewel.

"The boat is trolling, so it sometimes makes sudden moves like that," Cora told me. "It's okay. Try again. Hurry."

I nodded and swam to the rope. It was rough and wiry and totally inflexible. No wonder the girls couldn't sneak through. I glanced around at the holes to see if some were bigger than others. There was one that seemed a bit larger. It was going to be a tight fit, but I knew I could do it.

I squeezed my head in without too much of a problem and then wiggled around and got my body through. The rope scratched and burned my tail, but I ignored the pain and reached down. My fins were cut up and sore, but I remembered a trick from when I used to play hide-and-seek. I took a deep breath and folded my tail in half.

I was in!

"Jewel!" I cried and started shoving fish out of my way.

Jewel was crying. Her tail was tangled in the rope, and she couldn't swim away from it. Fish were pressed against each other, all of them struggling to get out and causing a bigger tangle.

I gritted my teeth and pressed through the fish to get to Jewel. I wrapped my arms around her and tugged, but she shrieked loudly when I pulled her. I had to get closer to get her tail loose.

Outside the net I heard the girls yelling, and our mothers' cries got louder and louder. I didn't pay attention. I had to focus on Jewel. As gently as I could, I unsnagged Jewel and then held her in my arms.

"Hey, little girl," I said and smiled to try to calm her down.

"Shyanna!" Cora called.

I looked through layers of fish at the holes in the thick rope as I held Jewel close. "You're moving,"

Cora cried, pointing up. “The net is being pulled to the surface. You need to hurry!”

I realized Cora was swimming higher as she yelled, her tail wiggling fast to keep up with the net as it was being pulled closer to the surface. Rachel was a few feet below her, swimming hard to try to catch up.

“Get out!” Cora shouted. “You have to get out before you reach the surface or the humans will see you!”

I squeezed through tons of little fish and dove toward the bottom of the net, holding Jewel tightly the entire time.

“The net is almost out of the water!” Cora cried. “No!”

Chapter Six

I put my head down and swam faster, protecting Jewel with my arms. I managed to squeeze through a wall of fish, and my head popped through a hole. I was going to make it! I pushed halfway through and was about to fold my fin to finish my escape from the net when Jewel screamed. Her torn tail was snagged on the wiry rope again.

I gently tugged her, trying to pull her through, but she cried louder. I glanced up in a panic. The rope was almost out of the water. I could see the reflection of the sun from below the water. We were close to the surface, and I was starting to panic.

I struggled to free Jewel without hurting her as we continued to move up. I held my breath. There was no way I was going to let her go on her own. Merpeople were yelling beneath us, but I didn't stop trying. I finally managed to pull her tail free, but a split second later realized that it was too late. The top of my head was already out of the water.

Around me, the fish gasped. They couldn't breathe out of the water, because they were unable to adapt to oxygen from air the way merpeople could. I closed my eyes and waited to be exposed. We were going to be pulled out of the water, and there was nothing I could do about it. It wouldn't be long before the fishermen realized they'd caught more than a net full of fish.

Humans still thought merpeople were just legends. Once the humans spotted us, we would be risking the underwater world and putting all

merpeople in jeopardy. The Kings and Queens of Mermaid Kingdom couldn't allow that to happen, which was why they had created a magic spell. If we were exposed to humans and were caught, we would lose our tails and memories of being mermaids. We would be human forever, never able to return to the ocean. It would seem as if the fishermen had caught a young human girl and a baby. If we were spotted but escaped, we would never be able to get legs. We would never be able to leave the ocean.

Everything was happening so quickly. I closed my eyes as I waited to be pulled to the surface. It was my thirteenth birthday. The day that was supposed to be the happiest day of my life. Instead, I was trapped in a net, about to be exposed to humans and lose my memories — and all of my family and friends.

With renewed energy and panic, I opened my eyes, dipped my head underwater, pulled on Jewel, and managed to force our way to the bottom of the net and out of a small hole.

Suddenly there were loud noises from the boat above us. Something was causing a huge commotion. There was shouting and waves, and then a beautiful sound that was a little muffled under the water. As quickly as it had begun, the commotion stopped.

The net dropped and went down fast. The top of the net opened as we sailed downward. I held tightly to Jewel and swam out, following a big, excited school of fish to safety. It was a miracle!

"We're free!" I shouted when we were outside the net. "We're safe, Jewel!"

I did a couple of victory flips, and Jewel stopped crying. She started to giggle. Then I swam over to Cora, who was watching us with wide eyes. I held out Jewel. Cora took her baby sister from me and hugged her close.

When she looked up at me, there were tears dropping down her cheeks. She blinked quickly as she stared at me and then looked up toward the surface of the water.

"I'm so sorry, Shy," she said.

"What's wrong?" I frowned and glanced at Rachel to see what was going on, but she was crying, too.

"Your mom . . ." Cora said.

That was the sound I'd heard.

A sound I hadn't heard in a very, very long time, since before my dad disappeared.

It was my mom, singing.

Chapter Seven

"What happened?" I demanded, feeling even more panicked than I had felt trapped in the net with Jewel.

Cora was holding Jewel close. "Your mom was very brave. She saved you. She saved you and Jewel." Cora's family and Rachel's dad were swimming closer to us, yelling my name and Jewel's. But all I could think about was my mom.

I glanced down at the ocean below from where they approached. Large strands of coral reef stretched up as if waving, and bright blue-cheeked butterflyfish swarmed around them, the scene colorful and deceptively beautiful. Up swam Cora's parents, their

eyes on Jewel, looking relieved and exhausted. But when they glanced at me, I saw the tears and sadness in their eyes. Cora's mom grabbed Jewel from Cora's arms, crying and holding her tightly.

"Oh, Shyanna, thank you," she whispered.

"Where's my mom?" I yelled at everyone and no one at the same time, with a bad feeling in my fins. I knew. I knew where she was, but nobody would say it.

"She said she was going to cause a distraction," Rachel's dad said quietly.

Cora's dad swam close to me and patted my arm gratefully. "Oh, Shyanna, you saved Jewel. You saved our baby."

"Where's my mom?" I shouted again, my dread growing as I looked around at all the beautiful sea life surrounding me.

"She said she was going to shock the fishermen so they'd drop the net," Rachel's dad said. "We couldn't stop her. She swam out of the water, and she started to sing."

"It was her," I whispered.

"It was the most powerful thing I've ever heard," Rachel's dad said, his eyes sad but filled with wonder. "I've never heard anything so beautiful in my life, and we were below the water. The humans above the water were so mesmerized that they dropped the net."

"But she didn't need to do that," I said. "I got free and saved Jewel."

"What a voice," Rachel's dad repeated, and everyone nodded solemnly.

I swallowed. "So my mom was seen by the humans? Singing?"

"She was," Rachel's dad said.

"And she's still up there?" I asked.

"No." We all turned to see Rachel. She was breathing heavily. "I swam up. She wasn't in the boat. They saw her, but she stayed on a rock and escaped before they broke out of their spell."

"Thank goodness!" I sighed with relief. I had been thinking the absolute worst. I knew she would never be able to use her legs again, but at least she was alive!

"She's trapped in the ocean now, forever," Rachel said sadly.

"Where is she?" I asked.

"The King and Queen are with her. They left the Neptunia Day celebrations and came right away," Rachel said.

"Already?" I asked. It seemed like it had all happened so quickly. It *had* all happened so quickly.

Rachel nodded. "The magic used is serious. They were here seconds later. They had to make sure Neptunia was safe."

"But she saved me. She saved Jewel," I whispered.

"I know," Rachel said. "But it's a big offense, Shy. Exposing herself to humans. She got away, but the King and Queen don't know if the humans realized what she was. They don't think anyone will believe the fishermen if they talk about what they saw. But rules are rules. She was seen. She'll never be able to use her legs on land again."

Chapter Eight

I swam up closer to the surface. The sunset was rippling over the water above, creating a gorgeous array of colors. There was no wind and no waves. It was totally still and quiet. The boat was gone. There was no sign of the King and Queen or my mom. It was eerie.

"They must have gone back to the palace," Rachel said.

"I have to get to her," I cried. "I have to see my mom!"

My shredded tail hurt from scraping the rope and folding up to escape, but I moved through the water faster than a shark on a hunt. I truly had never moved so fast in my life. Rachel and Cora were right behind me, swimming just as fast.

We swam through the gates of Neptunia, and immediately the festive sounds of Neptunia Day filled my ears.

The parade was over and night had fallen, but the celebrations would last until the last merpeople went to their caves. There was music and cheering coming from games and rides all over the castle, everything from sea horse racing to seaweed braiding to coral reef Ferris wheels. It was absolutely magical. I wish I could stop and enjoy it, but there wasn't time.

I swam straight to the castle, but the guard at the front raised his hand when I got near. “The King and Queen have asked you to stay away while they deal with your mother’s transgression,” he said in a deep, solemn voice.

“Come with us,” Cora’s mom said. I turned to see that Cora’s whole family and Rachel and her dad were right behind me. Cora’s mom was still clinging tightly to Jewel.

“We will all be at the Bell residence,” she said to the guard. “Please have the King and Queen inform

Shyanna's mother that we are gathered there, waiting for her. She's a hero."

We swam through the castle, swimming past merpeople old and young who were smiling and enjoying Neptunia Day festivities. No one seemed to notice the look on my face. They all smiled and waved.

Thankfully they had no idea what had happened. They had no idea that the entire Mermaid Kingdom was nearly exposed to the human world. If anyone found out, it would be complete chaos.

We swam inside Cora's family cave, and her mom disappeared to put the babies to bed while her dad made us some hot cocoa.

After I had the last sip of my cocoa, my mom came swimming into the living room. I swam up to meet her. She held out her arms, and I slipped inside.

"Oh, Mom," I said, sobbing. She'd saved me and Jewel from being exposed, and for that I was grateful. But I felt guilty. If only I could have saved Jewel faster none of this would have happened.

Mom patted my tangled hair, her arms tightly around me. "It's okay, honey," she whispered. "It's okay." I felt a little like a merbaby instead of a teenage mermaid.

"But you'll never walk on land again," I said. Tears ran down my cheeks like a waterfall.

"Oh, Shyanna," Mom said. "I haven't been on land for a long time anyhow."

"But you could go if you wanted to until now," I said. "And that's a big difference."

"It doesn't matter, Shy," she said. "It really doesn't matter much to me. I was so worried about you and baby Jewel being caught, and I couldn't lose you. I won't. Not you, too." She squeezed me tighter, and I knew we were both thinking about my dad.

I pulled back from her and looked into her eyes. "Your voice," I said. "Even from below, it was the most amazing sound. Rachel's dad said it was the most wonderful voice he's ever heard. And that's from a singing coach."

"That's an exaggeration," she said, blushing and looking shyly at the group.

"I don't think so," I told her. "Those humans were mesmerized. They didn't know what was happening. That's why they dropped the net." I hugged her tightly again and then pulled out of her arms. "Thank you, Mom. Thank you for saving us."

Cora's mom was crying. She swam over and embraced both of us. "It's my fault. I should have gone," Cora's mom said. "You saved my baby's life. And I did nothing."

My mom shook her head. "No. You were protecting the rest of your family. I was the closest to the surface. And my husband always used to tell me my voice could save us from humans if we were ever spotted. I've always been too shy, but he used to love going off on treasure hunts and singing. Oh, how he'd sing. He would sing day and night."

She stared off into space for a moment, remembering him. "It had to be me," she whispered.

Cora's dad swam over and circled all of us in his arms. We were all shedding salty tears, both happy and sad at the same time.

"Holy catfish!" Cora yelled, startling all of us out of our group hug.

We all stared at Cora. "Do you realize what time it is?" she cried again, pointing at the shell clock on the wall. "There's less than an hour until midnight!" she screamed. "And it's Shyanna's thirteenth birthday. We have to get her to shore!"

Everyone started talking at once.

"Oh my goodness, I didn't even get to make her shrimp cake!" my mom yelled.

"And her presents are still at home," Rachel called back.

"Never mind all that! It can wait. Her leg ceremony can't!" Cora pointed out. Thank goodness for Cora. She was always the sensible one.

My mom started to cry again. "I never even helped you pick out your song or outfit, and I missed our spa date." She hid her face in her hands. "I'm so sorry, Shyanna. I was so busy with the parade problems, and then all of this. And now I can't even take you on land."

"You saved my life, Mom," I said. "I forgive you."

"She's right. You saved my sister and your daughter, so we'll feel bad about her birthday party later," Cora said. "Right now, we need to focus on getting her to land."

"Maybe we should clean her up at a bit first," Rachel said nicely.

They all looked at me, and I looked down at myself. I was a mess. My manicure was in shreds, my hair was crazy, and my once-shimmering tail was tattered and torn up.

"No," I said quietly. "There isn't time."

"You're right," Rachel said. "It doesn't matter what you look like. I mean, you're beautiful, just a little . . . um . . . messy. All that matters is that you're there. On land. At midnight."

"No," I repeated, a little louder.

My mom put an arm around me. "The girls can go to land with you. I know it was supposed to be me. But it's okay. They are your best friends."

I shook my head again. "NO!" I said, even louder that time. Everyone stopped to stare at me.

"It's okay," I said. "I don't need to get my legs." Rachel and Cora's mouths dropped open. "If my mom doesn't get to leave the ocean, I don't want to either."

"But Shyanna," Rachel said. "You've been so excited about going on land. It's all you've been talking about for weeks."

"Years, actually," Cora said.

I crossed my arms and shook my head. "No. I don't want to go to land without my mom."

Rachel started to cry. "But Shyanna! You and Cora are my best friends, and land and legs are half of who I am. Cora and I have been waiting for you to turn thirteen so we could visit Owen on land together."

My mom swam forward and put both hands on my cheeks. She leaned her forehead up against mine. "No, Shy," she said. "Your dad would want you to go on land. He loved having legs. He loved taking me to shore. I hoped I'd go with you, but I can't. I won't let you miss out on that part of your life for me."

"But mom . . ." I started to say.

"No. I insist, Shyanna. Please. Do it for me. Do it for your dad." She let me go and swam over and put one arm around Rachel and the other arm around Cora. "Do it for your best friends. But mostly, do it for you. It's what you've always wanted, and you deserve it."

They all were staring at me. Watching me. Waiting.

"Fine," I finally said. "But there's something I have to do first, before we go to land. There's someone I need to talk to."

"Well, you better do it fast," Cora said.

"Follow me," was my reply as I quickly swam out the door.

Chapter Nine

I swam toward the royal courtyard. Rachel, Cora, my mom, and Rachel's dad followed me without speaking. Cora's parents needed to stay home with the girls.

Even though it was almost midnight, Neptunia festivities were still going strong. We quickly swam to the entrance.

"Will you wait here?" I asked my mom. She frowned but nodded, and Rachel's dad said he would wait with her.

Rachel, Cora, and I swam to the royal guard. I whispered to him what I was there to do.

He nodded and swam ahead, leading us into the courtyard. Rachel and Cora each took one of my hands, and we swam together to the Queen. When she spotted us, she left her royal guests and swam over to greet us. She smiled when she reached us.

"Your baby sister is okay?" she asked Cora.

Cora nodded and squeezed my hand.

"What you did today was brave," the Queen said to me. "Swimming into the net to get Jewel out." She nodded at all three of us. "You mergirls are a constant surprise to the kingdom. Great singers, great spirit, and great bravery."

"Thank you," we all said. I bowed my head. Beside me, Rachel and Cora did the same thing.

"I've come to ask a favor," I told the Queen as humbly as I could.

The Queen nodded. "It's about your mom?" she guessed.

I nodded. "Yes."

I took a deep breath before I continued. "I know she wasn't supposed to expose herself to humans, but we all know she only did it to save me. She saved me and baby Jewel from being exposed and captured. If she hadn't done that, I wouldn't be here — neither would baby Jewel.

The Queen nodded again. "I know, Shyanna. You are very lucky."

"Her voice saved us," I said. "It was beautiful. It's such a shame she hasn't sung in so long. It wasn't easy for her to do it. She hasn't sung since my dad . . ."

I lowered my eyes to the sand on the bottom of the ocean floor. The Queen glanced at the King, who was sitting in his throne juggling sea sponges while a group of admirers cheered.

"I would like to hear her sing sometime. Maybe I could even sing with her." She turned back to me. "Don't you have somewhere you're supposed to be?" She glanced at my messed-up tail and my crazy hairdo. I saw her hide a smile. “Tonight is your leg ceremony, isn’t it?”

“It’s supposed to be,” I told her.

She frowned ever so slightly.

“I was supposed to go to land with my mom,” I told her. “I would still love to do that. She’s all I have. I don’t have a dad anymore, and I don’t have any siblings. I only have my mom.”

The Queen sighed.

“Is there any way you can use magic?” I asked. “Can you reverse her spell so she can use her legs again? She saved two lives! It was a selfless act. There must be exceptions. Can you please help me? Please?” I begged.

The Queen clicked her tongue, glanced at the King again, and then back to me.

“I wish I could help you,” she said finally, “but I can’t reverse the spell that quickly. No one can. It has to be done in stages. Other royalty will need to help — if they agree at all. It would have to go to vote,

which takes time," she added and then looked into my eyes. "You must go, Shyanna. Time is ticking. It's midnight or nothing to get your legs. That spell can never be reversed."

Rachel and Cora each grabbed one of my hands again. I needed the support.

"But my mom," I said.

"Go on," the Queen said. "Go. Get your legs. I will discuss this matter with the King. I can't promise you anything. But we will discuss it, you have my word."

"Thank you," I said with a bow.

The girls pulled me away, but I glanced over my shoulder at the Queen as we left the courtyard. She was already at the King's side. He caught my eye and winked. I'd done what I could. Now it was time to go.

"Come on!" Cora said. "It's getting late. We are running out of time!"

Outside the castle, the girls let go of my hands, and my mom took one. "Is everything okay?" she asked me.

"I hope so," I whispered.

On the way to shore, Mom asked me what I'd planned for the leg ceremony. I told her all about my spa day and the plans I had made with Star. When I was finished, she started to sing. Goosebumps ran along my arms, down my back, and all the way down my tail. Her voice was simply incredible. Rachel's dad swam to my other side, and he joined in and sang with her. It was perfect.

As the song ended, we got close to the shore. Mom let go of my hand. "Go," she said. "I can't go any farther. Your friends will go with you."

Rachel's dad stayed with her, but Cora and Rachel swam up with me. The moonlight lit up the shore. It was breathtaking. There was a path of white flowers leading up the beach. I glanced at the girls.

"All of us came to do it earlier as a surprise," Rachel said. "Right before Jewel got trapped."

"So that's why you were all out? That's when Jewel got in the net. It was all for me?" I asked.

"Did you think we'd forget your birthday?" Cora asked. "Don't be silly!"

"Come on, Shy. It's time," Rachel said, smiling.

I breathed in the night air, nervous and excited about what was about to happen. And then I opened my mouth and began to sing.

I saw Rachel and Cora grin. It was our song. The song we first sang together at the Melody Pageant. The song that would always represent our friendship.

Rachel and Cora swam slowly beside me, and then they stepped out of the water. I blinked, and they had their legs. Lovely long, graceful limbs.

They walked up to the beach on the flower path and turned, waiting for me. I moved slowly forward. My tail began to tingle. It got heavier and heavier, and then a weird sensation ran down my middle. It didn't hurt. It just felt odd.

A breeze hit my legs, and I looked down and realized my tail was gone. I wore a bathing suit bottom, the same color and texture as my tail. But instead of a fin, I had feet. I had toes. I even had knees. I lifted one leg, shook it out a little, and began to laugh.

"Walk!" Rachel shouted, and they both clapped and called out encouragement. I tried to take another step and fell flat on my face.

"Exactly what I did!" Cora hollered. "Try again."

I laughed and got up on my knees.

"Try again!" Cora screamed. "It gets easier!"

Rachel ran farther up the beach. "Come on, Shyanna!"

I got up from my knees, wobbling a little and then finding balance on my feet.

"Wow!" I said. And then I took a step and then another. "I'm doing it!" I cried. "I'm walking."

"Oh, yes you are!" Cora ran to my side.

"Have fun, girls!" a voice called out from under the ocean.

My mom. I couldn't see her, but I knew she was there. Watching and smiling.

"Be back before morning," she yelled.

"We will," I shouted into the night air. The oxygen filled my lungs in a different way than the ocean water did. It made me light-headed, and I giggled and threw out my arms and kicked my new legs.

"It's too late for Owen to be here," Rachel told me. "But we'll come back soon. The three of us."

The three of us skipped together in the dark night air, enjoying every minute. Before I knew it, the sun was rising. I glanced down at my legs, wiggled my toes, and then stepped back into the ocean. There would be more adventures on another day.

I only hoped my mom would be able to be a part of them.

Chapter Ten

"Hey, sleepyhead!" a voice called from outside my room.

I opened my eyes, and memories of the day before rushed into my head. It hadn't been exactly the birthday I'd planned, but it was still the best birthday I could imagine. There was drama, excitement, adventure, and a happy ending.

I stretched my arms over my head and remembered the feeling of having legs. I wiggled my tail around, happy to have it back but eager to try out my new legs another time. It was completely indescribable.

"We were all up late, but you must have worn yourself out having such a great time on land!" Mom said. "You slept past noon. It's time to get up!"

"It was so fun, though, especially skipping," I told her, but then my heart sank a little, knowing she might never be able to go on land again.

"Legs are so different from a tail," she said, swimming into my room and doing a somersault. "Breathing air always made me so giggly."

I nodded, watching her. She didn't look sad, but my heart still ached a little for her.

"Come on, Shyanna," she said. "I'll make fish-shaped pancakes for breakfast!"

"Okay!" I swam out of bed and flipped around the room to find a comfortable shell top to change into. Then I followed her to the kitchen.

"SURPRISE!" voices yelled when I swam into the kitchen.

I screamed in shock, and everyone started to laugh. Our kitchen was full of merboys and mergirls and their parents.

"Happy belated birthday!" everyone shouted. I glanced around, my hand still on my heart.

"Today you get the party you were supposed to have yesterday!" my mom said as she swam to me and gave me a giant hug.

Rachel and Cora swam close. "With pancakes and presents!" Cora shouted.

"And shrimp cake," Rachel added.

Everyone was chattering and smiling. It was amazing. I blushed at a loud version of "Happy Birthday," and my heart came close to bursting with happiness. Then someone shoved me into a decorated shell chair, and someone else started handing me presents to open.

"Oh my gosh," I said. "Birthday presents!"

"We know how much you love presents!" Cora said and laughed.

"And we heard you saved Cora's baby sister," Cassie said. "That's amazing, Shyanna. You deserve lots of presents."

I glanced over at my mom. She put her finger on her lips to signal for me not to say anything about her role in the rescue of Jewel. Across the noisy room, our eyes locked for a moment and I smiled at her, so thankful to have her for my mom.

"How were your legs?" asked a classmate who hadn't yet turned thirteen as she handed me another gift to open.

"Magical," I told her. "Simply magical."

Everyone kept talking and laughing as I opened present after present, feeling like the luckiest mermaid in Mermaid Kingdom. As I was stuffing my face with another piece of shrimp cake, a hush went over the room. It went from noisy to quiet in a second. I turned from the table to see the Queen of Neptunia looking at me. She carried a scroll of paper in her hand.

I glanced behind her, but she was alone. No King or guard.

"Hello, Shyanna. I'm looking for your mom," she said formally. No one else in the room uttered a sound. Everyone's eyes were on the Queen. It was pretty surreal.

"Yes?" my mom said, looking confused. The crowd around me parted, and Mom floated in beside me and tucked my hand in hers, as if offering me moral support. I glanced at her face, but she looked calm, not as terrified and jumpy as I felt.

"I come with news," the Queen announced. She turned to me. "Shyanna Angler has come to me and requested special use of Mermaid Magic to reverse the spell that has taken away your ability to use your legs on land."

Merpeople around the room gasped, and a low whisper buzzed as they gossiped about what had happened. The Queen lifted her hand, and it went silent again.

"Last night, the King and I called an emergency session with the Royal Council to discuss this interesting situation."

I held my breath.

She stared at my mom. "We've reached a decision."

No one said a word. I didn't even hear anyone take a breath. The Queen waited an extra moment for dramatic effect. She loved to perform, the Queen. She cleared her throat and opened the scroll and began reading from it.

"The Royal Council has decided to grant Emerald Angler use of her legs, even though she was seen by humans."

Everyone in the room gasped and started whispering.

The Queen held up her hand and waited for quiet.

"It is because of special circumstances. Two mermaid lives were saved, and thus we have decided to alter the magic for leg use. But there will be strict stipulations."

I squeezed my mom's hand tightly. My heart pounded so loudly I was sure everyone in the room could hear it.

"Emerald will be allowed to use legs on land, but only when accompanied by either mermaid she saved, Shyanna Angler or Jewel Bass."

The room erupted in chatter again.

"She saved Jewel?" some people asked. "What happened? What humans saw her?"

The Queen was finished, and she rolled up the scroll and swam forward, ignoring the chaos in the room. She swam to my mom and me, smiled, and handed over the scroll to my mom.

"What you did was very brave. I see where your daughter gets her bravery," the Queen said to my mom. She winked at me.

"I would like to hear you sing sometime," she said to my mom. "Perhaps a duet?"

My mom nodded quickly, and the Queen smiled and bowed her head.

"Thank you so much," I told her. I grinned. "Can I offer you and the King a slice of birthday cake? You can take it back to him."

"Salmon cake?" she asked.

"Shrimp," I told her.

"The King and I love a good shrimp cake," she said and patted my head.

I got her two large pieces and wrapped them up. When I finished, the Queen was laughing with my mom about something. I handed her the cake. "Thank you again," I said.

She accepted the cake. "The King is sorry he couldn't come along. He had a round of sea golf booked with another king and couldn't get out of it." She smiled brightly. "Try and stay out of trouble now, Shyanna," she said.

And then she was gone.

Mom put her mouth close to my ear. "After the party is over, you and I are going to land," she whispered.

"Are you sure?" I asked. It would be her first time on land since my dad disappeared.

"It's time," she said.

Rachel and Cora swam over to squeal with me. I looked at my mom. "Is it okay if my best friends come?"

She nodded. "I wouldn't want it any other way. These girls are like family!"

I told Rachel and Cora what we were going to do, and then we twirled in circles and did flips of excitement.

It was the best belated birthday party anyone had ever had. Even my biggest dreams couldn't compare. All of my wishes had come true.

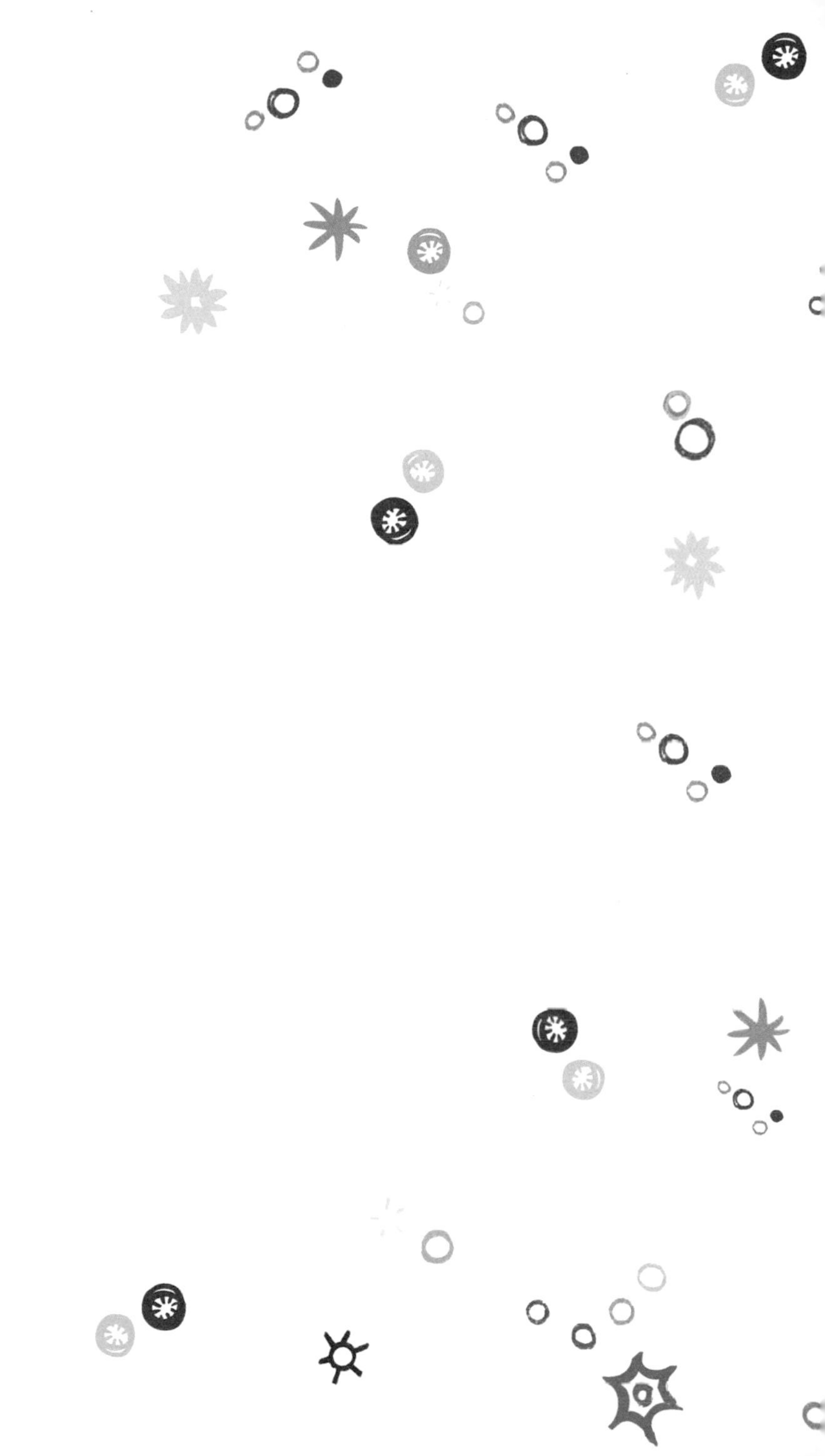

Part Two: Rachel's Tale

Chapter Eleven

My stomach hurt from worrying about my best friend, Owen, a human I'd met onshore when I lived at Caspian Castle. I could tell something was wrong with him, and I needed to find out what so I could try to help him feel better.

I chomped on my lip like it was a salty seaweed snack as my friend Shyanna and I swam out of Walrus Waterpark. Cora, our other friend, had left a few minutes earlier, swimming off in the opposite direction.

Shyanna giggled as we swam past a bloom of jellyfish. Her beautiful tail sparkled and reflected off their translucent skin. She waved at them and then turned back to me. When she saw my face, her expression softened. "What's wrong, Rachel?" Shyanna asked.

"To tell the truth, I'm worried about Owen," I told her.

Shyanna stopped swimming. "What's wrong with Owen? Is he sick? Does he have one of those human diseases like chicken pox? Wait. Has he been around chickens? Have you ever seen real live chickens? They're as cute as sea cucumbers."

I was too troubled to even smile at Shyanna's excitement. "He's not sick, but Owen hasn't come to visit Neptunia in a long time, even though he can, thanks to the special merman powers the King and Queen granted him. And when I go to shore to visit, he doesn't seem happy to see me," I told her.

"Did you ask him what's wrong?" Shy asked.

My cheeks heated up. I hadn't. I'd been trying to think if I'd done something wrong, something to make him mad. I sighed. "I'm kind of afraid to."

Shyanna swam close and hugged me. "You need to ask, Rachel," she said. "Talk to him. And it's Friday so you're going to see him today, right?"

"Yeah," I said with a nod. Every Friday I swam to shore and visited Owen. Since I was half-human, I could go on land whenever I wanted and change back to a mermaid anytime.

"So ask!" she said.

As if sensing my gloomy mood, a clown fish flipped around in front of me, trying to make me laugh. I smiled but glanced toward the exit of our castle. "I'm heading to Platypus Island now," I said.

"Alone?" Shyanna asked. "I wish I could come, but I'm meeting my mom at the Fish Factory, and then we're going to visit Pearl Sparkles."

I nodded. "It's okay. I have a route worked out. It's fast and safe, and I've never run into trouble."

Shyanna frowned for a moment. "Okay, but be careful," she warned me. Then she grinned her warm, friendly smile and patted my shoulder. "And try not to be nervous. If you ask Owen, I'm sure he'll tell you what's wrong."

I nodded. Swimming to shore alone didn't worry me. I'd done it enough times by now. It was Owen who worried me. I hoped Shyanna was right and once I talked to him, everything would go back to normal.

I waved goodbye to Shyanna and swam out the gates of Neptunia. Before I knew it, I'd reached the Octopi guards outside Platypus Island. They nodded as I passed. They were used to seeing me heading to shore to visit.

My stomach fluttered with nerves as I neared the shoreline. My head poked through the top of the water, and my lungs switched to breathing in oxygen from air rather than the water. As I reached shallow water, I felt pebbles on my tail. It began to tingle and transform, and in moments, human legs took its place. I now wore shorts the same color as my fin, and I stood up and ran to grab the shoes I'd stored behind a bush close to the beach.

Excitement mixing with worry gave me a burst of energy, and I ran faster than usual toward my meeting spot with Owen. A smile tugged up my lips up as I ducked around branches, climbing over rocks and sticks. The scent of the trees and grass, so different from the ocean, filled my nose.

Finally I reached the spot where Owen met me on Fridays. I crossed my fingers, hoping he'd be back to his happy self — or at least trust me enough to tell me what was bothering him.

I parted the branches and stepped through. Our meeting place was empty.

Nothing. No sign of Owen.

I walked farther out in the field, wondering if he was running late. But Owen was never late. I glanced around again, but he was nowhere to be seen.

My mouth began to quiver. Owen wasn't showing up. He didn't want to talk to me. I swallowed and thought about going out after him. But he hadn't shown up. I couldn't chase after him. If he'd wanted to talk to me, he'd have come to meet me.

The minutes ticked by slowly, and my body felt heavier with every passing second. I sat on a big rock, waiting, but Owen never came.

Chapter Twelve

A shark held Owen between his teeth. I held his leg, pulling as hard as I could, but I couldn't manage to free him.

"OWEN!" I yelled.

Suddenly there was a huge thump, followed by pain in my tail. My eyes flew open. I'd flipped myself right off my bed and landed on the floor. I'd been asleep; it was just a nightmare.

I sighed as reality roared into my sleepy head. Owen had stood me up! He didn't like me anymore.

I swallowed and swam up from the floor, trying to think happy mermaid thoughts, but it was no use. I was as blue as a hundred-foot whale.

"Rachel!" Dad called from outside my bedroom. "The mergirls are here. Are you awake? Can I send them up?"

I rubbed the sleep out of my eyes. "Sure!" I replied. Almost as soon as the word was out of my mouth, Shyanna and Cora raced into my room.

"Hey, sleepyhead," Shyanna said, laughing. "How come you're still in bed?"

"I slept in," I said. "I couldn't get to sleep last night." I swam toward my door to avoid giving more detail. "Come on, I'm starving. Let's go to the kitchen and get some food. I'm sure my dad made extra breakfast."

Shyanna sped up beside me and bumped my fin with hers. "So?" she said pointedly. "How did it go with Owen? Is everything okay between you guys now?"

My lip trembled. I swallowed, but it felt like a piece of coral was stuck in my throat. Ignoring Shyanna's question, I hurried to the kitchen where, as expected, Dad was frying up breakfast. Shrimp fries. Enough for all of us.

Dad lifted his spatula in a wave when we entered. "Hey, mergirls, I hope you're hungry," he said.

"Always!" Shyanna said.

Cora swam close to me and tapped me on my shoulder. "What's wrong, Rachel?"

My lips wobbled and tears threatened to spill out. I waved my hands in front of my face, trying to smile even though I wanted to cry. Dad watched me, looking worried.

"What happened?" Shy asked. "Did something happen during your trip to shore yesterday?"

"Is something wrong with Owen?" Cora asked, sounding concerned.

"What's wrong with my favorite daughter?" Dad asked at the same time.

Cora and Shyanna each reached for one of my hands and squeezed it. Dad watched, flipping over the shrimp. I couldn't even enjoy the delicious smell of the special breakfast he'd made. Sadness made my tail droop.

"Owen didn't show up," I said, and a tear slipped out. Shyanna quickly reached for it and held it in her hand, then grabbed a container to slip my tear inside. Mermaid tears are full of mermaid magic, so it was important not to waste a single one.

Cora, Shyanna, and my dad all started firing off questions at once:

"Did you go to his house?"

"Did you look for him?"

"Why didn't you tell me?"

I shook my head and refused to look at any of them. "He obviously didn't want to see me, so I wasn't going to make it worse by chasing all over after him." My chin dropped to my chest as I finally faced the truth I'd been trying to avoid. "He doesn't like me anymore, and he clearly doesn't want to be my friend."

My dad scoffed at that. "What's not to like?" He swam over to the cupboard and grabbed some shell plates. Then he swam quickly back to the stove to start dishing out breakfast.

"Exactly," Shyanna said, swimming over to help my dad set out some Plant Life veggies on the plates. "He's your best friend, Rachel. You've known him longer than you've known us, and we love you more with every passing day!"

Cora swam over to help my dad too. "Owen loves when you visit him onshore. Especially on Friday. He told Justin that."

I glanced over and saw her cheeks turn a little pink. Justin was one of Owen's human friends. We'd met him when we'd visited Owen on land, and it seemed like Cora had developed a bit of a crush on him. She turned quickly away and grabbed a jug of clam juice.

"And Owen loves visiting the ocean too," Cora continued. "You're his best friend, and he's yours. Well, along with me and Shy." She smiled as she put out shell cups for the clam juice.

Dad clapped his hands together. "All right! Let's eat." He pointed at the feast on the table. "Rachel, you're too hard on yourself. Owen's a special human and getting to use a mertail is really important to him — as are you. It has to be something else. Did you two have a fight?"

I shook my head. "No. That's the thing. I can't pinpoint anything. I've gone over it and over it, but he's been acting funny for a few weeks. Maybe he doesn't like the fact that I'm a mermaid anymore. Maybe he doesn't want friends like me. I'm so different from all his other human friends."

"Nonsense," Shyanna, Cora, and my dad all said at the same time. If I weren't so worried, I'd have thought it was kind of funny the way they kept talking in sync.

"Listen, Rachel, I know you're sensitive, but Owen thinks you're the catfish's meow," Cora added.

"Not anymore," I muttered, hanging my head again.

"Maybe he was in an accident," Shyanna suggested.

"More likely he got in trouble, and his parents wouldn't let him go out," Dad said. "Swim up to the table, mergirls, and fill up your plates."

Cora loaded her plate. "Let's all go to shore. We can ask Justin if he knows anything. Um, I mean, we can talk to his friends. We'll find out what's going on. We can make lots of guesses, but how well do we really understand human behavior?" She shoved a huge mouthful of shrimp into her mouth and giggled. "Mmm. This is delicious, Mr. Marlin."

I shoved a shrimp into my own mouth and watched Cora. I had a sneaking suspicion her desire to go back to shore had something to do with Justin.

"It is a good idea," Shyanna agreed. "Thanks for cooking for us, Mr. Marlin." She helped herself to a large helping of Plant Life with her shrimp and turned to me. "Let's go get an answer."

"But we're supposed to go play with the dolphins later," I pointed out. "And I know how much you love that."

"It's okay," Shy said. "We need to find out what's really going on with Owen. There's no way he doesn't want to be your friend anymore. That makes no sense at all."

I glanced at my dad. He nodded. "It's okay with me, but you mergirls better check with your mothers," he said to my friends. "After we finish our feast."

We all ate up, and I listened halfheartedly as my friends chatted with my dad about what Queen Kenna was up to these days. Nerves flipped around my stomach, and I could barely follow along.

After we'd cleaned up, Cora and Shyanna took out their shell phones to call their caves.

"Please, Mom," Cora begged when it was her turn. "It's really important that I go to shore to help

Rachel. I can ask Cassie to look after baby Jewel." She listened and then hung up the shell phone and looked at me, a little panic in her eyes.

"You sure seem anxious to go to shore," my dad said with a wink.

"For Rachel, of course," Cora said. "I'm supposed to babysit because my mom is taking my other sisters to the merdoctor, and my dad is working." Cora dialed again and breathed a sigh of relief when Cassie agreed to babysit. Then she called her mom back and told her the good news.

"I don't have long," Cora said when she finally hung up for good. "I have to be back in two hours, or I'm in the trouble of my life. Like huge."

"No problem," I told her. "That gives us lots of time. I promise."

"Okay!" Shyanna said, swimming to my side and linking arms with Cora and me. "We're all set."

Dad swam with us to the front of the cave and watched us swim off. "Have fun, mergirls!" he called.

"Swim safe, and, Rachel, remember to check the time when you're on land, so you don't overstay your visit! You don't want to get Cora in trouble when she's doing you a favor by going to shore with you."

"I won't, Dad!" I called back. As a half-human, I could stay onshore as long as I wanted, while Shyanna and Cora could be on land as long as forty-eight hours before their tails grew back. But despite all that, Cora had limited time. We needed to get home in two hours. I'd promised.

"Come on," Cora said. She sped out in front of us and did a figure eight so quickly her purple tail was a blur. "Let's go find out what's wrong with Owen."

Chapter Thirteen

We raced through the ocean, passing by other castles and occasionally seeing other merboys and mergirls we recognized. We waved but kept moving quickly so they wouldn't swim over to say hello. I didn't want to waste any of our precious time.

But suddenly I spotted a problem. Up ahead, only about one hundred feet away, there was a frenzy of short-fin mako sharks swimming in circles.

"Oh, no!" I cried, my eyes going as wide as sand dollars. "Look!"

"Come on," Shyanna said. She grabbed my hand and quickly darted behind a giant blue whale. Cora swam close behind. The whale blinked kindly, and we rubbed up against him while the sharks swam closer and closer.

I held my breath, terrified. These were the same kind of sharks that had killed my mom years ago. Ocean life was truly breathtaking, but it was also dangerous.

Once, when Shyanna had gone to shore looking for a magical cure for her sore throat, we'd swum straight into a pack of sharks. She'd had to rescue me when I froze as the sharks approached, their pointed teeth bared. Shyanna had made me sing with her, and the blend of our voices had mesmerized the sharks and saved our lives.

"I'm so glad I haven't run into them again since that last time with you," I whispered to Shyanna as our new whale friend kept us camouflaged and safe from harm.

Fortunately, this time the sharks swam off without spotting us. "This is why I worry about you when you come to shore alone," Shyanna told me.

We thanked the whale and promised to bring him some special krill the next time we came to shore, then swam off toward Platypus Island.

As soon as we got close to the beach, I spotted Owen and his friends, Justin, Mitchel, and Morgan, standing in the field just past the tree line that separated the land from the beach. The boys were kicking around a black-and-white ball on the grass. I looked at Owen's face from the distance. He wore a giant smile, which made my heart both happy and sad. He never looked like that when he looked at me these days, but at least he was happy now!

"That's a soccer ball," Cora whispered. She loved all water sports in the ocean and had made it her mission to learn about all the human ones ever since she'd gotten her legs on her thirteenth birthday and started coming to shore with me.

Shyanna, Cora, and I tried not to make any noise as our tails tingled, and we got our legs. Then we all grabbed the shoes we kept stashed onshore and started through the trees.

"Shhh," Cora whispered as she took off in the lead. She was the fastest swimmer and the fastest on land too. "Let's sneak up and surprise them." Her eyes sparkled like stars above the ocean.

We crept closer, and all at once Cora emerged from the tree line. "Boo!" she shouted.

I hung back a little, watching Owen's reaction. His eyes immediately met mine, and for a moment, he dropped his gaze. When he glanced up again, he was smiling, but the usual spark wasn't in his eyes. My stomach flopped like a flappy fish.

Cora jumped up as high as she could with gravity and legs instead of water and a tail. Shyanna jumped too, and both of them whooped out loud, caught up in the excitement of being on land with humans — cute boy ones at that.

Cora ran straight for the black-and-white ball and kicked it high in the air.

“Nice kick!” Justin shouted, taking off after the ball.

Cora giggled and blushed, proving that my hunch was right. She had a crush on him!

I smiled and watched as Morgan and Owen chased after Justin. Cora followed. With an apologetic glance at me, as if she couldn’t help herself, Shyanna took off running too. Mitchel whooped and then followed behind her.

I stayed close to the tree line and quietly watched the fun. The girls tried to keep up, but the boys raced around them, passing the ball to one another using their feet.

I didn’t mind that Shyanna and Cora were playing along. There was still time to talk to Owen. Besides, it didn’t look like the boys were in any hurry to stop and talk. Owen glanced at me from time to time, but he didn’t come over.

Finally Justin kicked the ball close to me and raced after it, his brownish-blond hair standing straight up in the wind. His nice white teeth flashed a delighted grin as he ran toward me. He looked as happy and friendly as a dancing dolphin.

I stepped out of his way and saw Owen running closer to me, closing in on Justin from behind. Cora screeched, trying to catch up. I glanced over at her, and when I looked back, Owen was standing right in front of me, panting and out of breath.

"Uh . . . I'm really sorry I couldn't make it yesterday, Rachel," Owen said. He glanced away, his eyes following the ball as Justin kicked it high in the air. "I wanted to let you know so you wouldn't come all that way for nothing, but uh . . . I had no way of reaching you."

Owen shuffled his feet a little and stared down at the grass. "Our Internet doesn't exactly work in the ocean, and I can't reach you on a shell phone." He lifted a shoulder and shrugged as if it were no big deal. As if it didn't much matter to him one way or the other.

I waited for more. For him to tell me why he couldn't make it, why he was acting so distant, why he didn't like me anymore. But Owen turned away without a second glance and took off after the ball.

I stared after him, feeling like my heart had been pierced by a fishhook.

Chapter Fourteen

A few minutes later, Cora ran close to me. She stopped and bumped my hip with hers. "So you and Owen talked and now everything's okay?" she said. She didn't really seem to be listening for my answer. She was too busy watching Justin and the ball. She seemed to have forgotten all about her offer to talk to the other boys and help me figure out what was wrong with Owen.

I shrugged, but Cora grabbed my hand and pulled me, running so I had no choice but to follow to keep up. "Come on, this game is so much fun!" she exclaimed.

I dropped Cora's hand and came to a halt on the grass as she chased after her crush. Now I felt even worse. Cora didn't care, and Owen didn't care. What was wrong? Was it me? Was I doing something to make my friends turn away from me?

Just then, Shyanna hurried over to my side. "Are you okay, Rachel?" she asked. "Did you and Owen talk? Is everything okay? He told you what's wrong, right?"

I shook my head, feeling miserable. Shy and I both looked over to where Owen was running, his head thrown back with laughter.

"But he seems fine," Shyanna said. "He doesn't seem mad at you. I mean, yeah, he's obviously into the soccer game right now, but you know he loves sports. He's like Cora. He gets caught up and forgets everything else."

I nodded, wishing she were right.

"Come on!" Shyanna encouraged. "Join in the fun. Everything's okay!"

I wanted to believe her, but my heart didn't agree. "I don't know," I said cautiously, but Shyanna ignored my protests and pulled me into the game.

I halfheartedly joined in and kept an eye on Owen. He seemed to run off in the opposite direction whenever I got close enough to talk to him. Something was definitely off, and I seemed to be the only person who could see it. Or maybe I was just the only person Owen wasn't happy around.

"Let's take a break," Justin suggested after awhile. He plunked down on the grass, and everyone else followed his lead.

I moved closer to Owen and sat down next to him, but he quickly jumped up to grab the soccer ball. When he sat back down, he made sure to do it on the other side of the circle. I plucked up some grass in my hand and squished the blades between my fingers, noticing how my fingers turned green.

"Our swim team is going to the championships next weekend," Justin announced.

"Our club has a good chance to win the Castle . . . um . . . championships," Cora said. Unlike Owen, the rest of the boys had no idea we were mermaids.

"Wait a minute, I thought you girls didn't swim," Morgan said. "I've never seen any of you in the ocean. I thought you were afraid of the water."

Cora's eyes opened wide, realizing her mistake.

Luckily, Mitchel didn't seem to notice anything out of the ordinary. "You wanna race?" he asked with a smile.

Cora, Shyanna, and I exchanged nervous glances. We couldn't race the boys. In fact, as mergirls, we couldn't swim in front of humans at all. As soon as we were in water, our legs would disappear and our glorious sparkly tails would be on display. Other than Owen, who had special permission from the King and Queen of Neptunia and knew about mermaids, humans were not allowed to see our tails.

"Uh . . ." Cora said. "I can't. I . . . uh . . . I thought you meant um . . ." she appeared to be searching for the right word.

"Did you mean your track team?" Owen said quietly.

"Yeah, exactly," Cora agreed quickly, glancing down at her legs. She stretched them out in front of her and wiggled them around. "I was talking about running track. The running championships."

"Yeah?" Justin grinned his playful grin and jumped to his feet. "I'll race you."

Shyanna and I both shook our heads, but Cora's gaze was focused on Justin. She jumped up, unable to resist a challenge.

"Cora," Shyanna said warningly. We both knew Cora wasn't nearly as fast on her legs as she was with her tail. She hadn't been thirteen for very long and was still getting used to her legs.

But there was no stopping Cora. She was off and running, and Justin took off after her. They hadn't gone far when suddenly we heard a loud crunch, and then Cora dropped to her knees, yelling and grabbing at her leg.

"Ow!" Cora yelped as the rest of us jumped up and ran over. When Justin noticed she wasn't behind him anymore, he turned and quickly ran back to her.

Cora rubbed at her leg. "It's nothing," she said, but it was obvious from the look on her face that it hurt — a lot. She tried to stand up and walk but collapsed to the ground.

I glanced up. The sun was quickly moving east. We'd lost some time when we'd hidden from the sharks, and we needed to start moving to get Cora home on time. If she was late, she wouldn't be coming back to the shore for a long, long time. She'd be devastated.

"Just sit and rest for a while before you try to move," Justin said.

Shyanna caught my eye. "We have to get going soon," she said, a nervous crack in her voice. "Cora has a curfew."

"We'll walk you home," the boys offered. Mitchel and Morgan each took one of Cora's arms and helped lift her to her feet.

Shyanna and I looked at each other. The boys couldn't walk us home — not to Mermaid Kingdom — and we couldn't let them see where we were going.

"No, it's okay," Shyanna said. "We'll take her." We tried to force them out of the way, but they didn't let go of Cora.

I glanced at the sun again. We really did need to get to the shore. We didn't have time to wait for Cora's foot to feel better, and we couldn't let the boys come with us to the ocean. They'd see the truth.

I glanced at Owen. "Help," I mouthed.

Owen smiled, and in that moment, he looked just like my old friend. My heart sped up. It was the first time he'd looked at me like that in weeks. Maybe things would be okay after all.

"Hey, guys," Owen said to his friends. "The girls are fine. Let them head back together."

Justin shook his head. "No, we should make sure she's okay."

Cora smiled at him and shook the other boys off her arms. "I'm fine. I can walk."

Owen winked at me. "Come on, guys. We should head to my place. My mom made us a chocolate forest cake."

"My favorite!" Justin exclaimed. The other boys cheered with excitement. With the promise of food, they all took off running in the direction of Owen's house — away from the ocean.

Owen glanced back at me. I stared at him, unable to keep the hurt off my face. He paused, and for a moment I thought he was going to tell me something, but then he waved. "See you!" he called, running after his friends.

I wanted to cry. We still hadn't had a chance to have a real talk with Owen! But instead, I turned to Cora. "Can you walk?" I asked. "We have to get you home."

Cora put one arm over my shoulder and one arm over Shyanna's, and we hobbled along, moving slowly.

"Um, Rachel," Cora asked, "if something happens to my leg, does it affect my tail?"

"I have no idea," I snapped at her. "But if we don't get you home, you might not see Justin for a long time."

Cora stopped hobbling for a second. "You and Owen worked things out, right?"

I didn't answer.

"Oh, Rachel," Cora said, her voice cracking. "I'm so sorry. I got so caught up . . . "

"Flirting with Justin?" I said.

Cora dropped her head. "I'm sorry. I completely forgot to ask the other boys about what's going on with Owen."

"It's okay," I told her. "It's not your fault. Owen's problem is with me. Now let's get you home before you get into trouble."

Chapter Fifteen

Thankfully, we made it home on time — and without running into any more sharks! The first thing my dad asked was how things had gone with Owen. I tried to convince him — and myself — that everything was fine. If Owen didn't want to be my best friend anymore, well, I had the mergirls and the Spirit Squad 2 and lots of new friends in Neptunia! It wasn't the end of the ocean!

The next morning, Dad gave me a hug and then headed off to see the Queen after breakfast. He was her singing instructor. I swam out into the yard just as Cora swam up. She had Jewel with her, and I couldn't help grinning at how cute my friend's baby sister was.

"Wow!" I said, admiring Cora's beautiful turquoise shell top. It made her colorful purple tail dazzle. "You look pretty beautiful to be babysitting."

"Thanks," Cora replied, blushing and looking away.

For a few minutes, we watched Jewel babble to a couple of sea starfish on the ocean ground. Finally Cora looked up at me. "So . . . are you sure you're not mad at me?" she asked. "I'm really sorry for not even trying to talk to the boys about Owen for you."

"It's okay," I told her. I didn't really want to talk about it. "How's your tail?"

"It seems fine. Maybe a little bruised where I hurt my leg but hardly noticeable."

"Good," I said. I grinned mischievously and sang: "Justin and Cora sitting in a tree . . ." I stopped quickly and smiled to show I was teasing.

Cora blushed again. "We're friends!" she said but played with her hair nervously. "Actually he kind of asked me . . . us . . . to go shell hunting today. The boys are searching for a rare red dwarf mussel shell, the same shell Shyanna found."

I glanced over at the sea starfish and Jewel. The starfish lifted an arm and watched us with the eye on the end.

"I told him I'd help. I know where to find one! Do you want to come?" Cora asked. "This time I'll make sure we talk to Owen and get to the bottom of things."

"When did Justin ask you along for the shell hunt?" I asked, trying to pretend I wasn't hurt that Owen hadn't invited me.

"When we were playing soccer," Cora replied. She glanced down, and her cheeks flushed until they were as red as a lobster tail.

As much as I wanted to show how good I was at shell hunting too, I couldn't face Owen again today. I didn't want to risk more disappointment. Besides, he hadn't even invited me. Things were weird, and I wasn't about to beg him to talk to me if he didn't want to.

I shook my head. "I really can't, Cora. I'm sorry. Why don't you ask Shyanna? She'll go," I said.

Cora shook her head. "She's with her mom today. They're taking a singing lesson with your dad and the Queen."

"Oh, that's right," I said. "I forgot. He's meeting them at Queen Kenna's."

Cora reached out and touched my arm. "Please don't be sad, Rachel. Owen still likes you. I know it. You should really come and talk to him. Clear things up once and for all."

I swam closer to watch baby Jewel and the sea starfish. "No. I don't want to deal with it today." I glanced at Cora. "Do you need me to babysit for you?" I wondered if that's why she really came over.

Cora shook her head. "No, Cassie said she would."

That made me feel a little bit better. At least Cora really did want me to go with her. She wasn't just trying to get me to look after her sister so she could go to shore and see Justin.

"I only have two hours again," Cora continued. "I have to hunt fast." She frowned. "I hate seeing you like this. You should come."

My bottom lip trembled. My feelings were already hurt, and I didn't want to keep trying to fix things if Owen didn't want to. Besides, it's not like he couldn't use mermaid magic to visit me if he wanted to.

At that moment Jewel stuck her finger out and the starfish squealed as it tried to scurry away. Jewel's mouth formed into an O, and she giggled. It was the cutest sound. Like Shyanna, sometimes I was envious of Cora's sisters.

"Why don't you ask Cassie to go to shore with you instead?" I suggested. "I don't mind babysitting Jewel. In fact, I'd love to. She's just what I need today. I can pretend to be a big sister."

"Trust me, baby sisters aren't all they're cracked up to be," Cora said. "You have so much freedom."

"Things always look bluer . . ." I started to say.

"On the other side of the ocean," Cora finished with a smile.

"Go show off for Justin," I said. The look on Cora's face made me giggle. She was glowing like plankton. "Be careful of those short-fin mako sharks."

Cora waved her hand. "They'll be long gone. Besides, you go to Platypus Island alone all the time."

"Yeah, because I've been doing it longer," I said. "I know all the shortcuts and hiding spots in case of danger. You haven't had your legs for very long."

Cora flipped her hair. "I'll swim by Cassie's cave on the way and see if she wants to join me. She's been wanting to meet our human friends." Cora swam down and kissed Jewel on top of her head. "You're sure you don't mind?"

"Go on," I said. "You don't have a lot of time if you're going to impress the boys with your mad hunting skills!"

Cora swam off, an extra wiggle in her tail.

* * *

Baby Jewel was adorable. We played with the starfish, and then I took her inside for a snack. She ended up taking a nap right at the kitchen table! When she woke up, I took her to Walrus Waterpark. I made sure to leave a note for Cora at my cave so she'd know where to find us.

Cora could say what she wanted about being a big sister, but playing with Jewel definitely kept my mind off Owen. I chased her down the slide and pushed her in the baby swing. Later we were joined in the park by a young merboy and mergirl from nearby caves. They were obviously best friends — I could tell by the way they played and finished each other's sentences. Seeing them, my heart ached a little. They reminded me of Owen and me.

When I looked down at my shell watch, I was shocked how much time had passed. I glanced around the water park. Cora should be back by now. I kept an eye on the entrance to the water park, but there was no sign of her.

I started to get worried, remembering the sharks. I pulled my shell phone out and called Cassie's cave. She answered right away. "Are you guys back already? Is Cora with you?" I asked.

"Cora? No. She went to shore to play with those human boys," Cassie said.

"I thought you went with her?" I said.

"My mom wouldn't let me," Cassie answered.

I tried not to sound nervous as I said goodbye and hung up. My shell phone rang almost immediately.

"Rachel. It's Mrs. Bass," Cora's mother said when I picked up. "Is Cora with you? She needs to get home right away."

I glanced around, but there was still no sign of Cora. Where was she, and what was taking her so long?

Chapter Sixteen

"Um, Cora isn't back yet, Mrs. Bass," I said into the shell phone. "I'm sure she's on her way. I know she was going shell hunting. She probably just lost track of time." I didn't mention the sharks we'd seen the day before — or that Cora had gone shell hunting alone. "Do you want me to bring Jewel home?"

As if on cue, Jewel started to cry, signaling that playtime was over. I tried to shush her and gave her a reassuring smile.

"Yes, please," Mrs. Bass replied. "I'll see you soon."

I hung up the shell phone, rocked Jewel gently in my arms, and swam toward Cora's cave. She was asleep by the time we arrived. Cora's mom and dad swam out of their cave to meet me.

"Still no sign of Cora?" Mrs. Bass asked as she took Jewel from my arms. "She's with Cassie, isn't she?"

I didn't answer, and her mom handed Jewel to her husband. "Can you put Jewel in her crib, dear?" she asked.

Cora's dad nodded and smiled at me, then took the baby from his wife and swam back inside.

"I'm worried, Rachel," Mrs. Bass said. "Cora isn't usually late. She knows how strict I am about curfews. This isn't like her." She glanced at their cave. "We're supposed to visit Grandmermaid." She looked down at the large shell watch on her wrist. "She knows it's important to me to be on time."

"Well . . . you know how competitive Cora is," I said. "Maybe she had trouble finding the shell but wanted to show off a little."

I thought about the mako sharks, and my worry started to grow. I didn't say anything about Cora's crush on Justin and how that might have distracted her from her curfew. And I didn't mention that Cassie hadn't gone with her or that Cora had hurt her leg the day before. I didn't know if mermaid legs healed quickly or not. If she got stuck onshore it would be a disaster. I should have made sure Cassie was allowed to go before I offered to babysit Jewel.

"I'll go and see what's going on," I told Cora's mom. "I'm sure she's on her way back, but I can go meet her, just to make sure nothing's wrong."

"Is Cassie with her?" her mom asked again.

I couldn't lie. I shook my head, and Cora's mom frowned. "I'll go with you," she said. "I don't want you going off on your own too. I really wish Cora hadn't done that. She certainly won't be allowed to in the future."

The two of us had just started swimming toward the exit of Neptunia Castle when, in a whirl of bubbles and motion, Cora raced inside. Her eyes were wide, and when she glanced at me they grew even bigger.

"Cora Bass," her mom said. "You are late. You had us worried." I knew Mrs. Bass was relieved Cora was okay, but that wouldn't get Cora out of the big trouble she was in.

"Rachel —" Cora started to say.

"Cora," her mom interrupted, "come back to the cave with me right now." She motioned for her daughter to start moving. "You are not going to leave our cave until it's time to go back to school." Mrs. Bass glanced at me. "Thank you for looking after Jewel. Now move it, Cora."

"But I have to tell Rachel —" Cora started to say, looking at me.

"Cave," Mrs. Bass said firmly, pointing in the direction of their home. "And no shell phone and no talking to your friends for the rest of the weekend. You'll wait until school."

"But . . ." Cora looked at me, her eyes wide. There was an expression on her face that I couldn't quite figure out.

"No," her mother said, crossing her arms until Cora started to swim.

Just before they disappeared from sight, Cora turned back to look at me over her shoulder. "I HAVE SOMETHING IMPORTANT TO TELL YOU," she mouthed.

I frowned. I was as curious as a catfish, but I'd have to wait until Cora's punishment was over to find out what was so important. What had she discovered?

Chapter Seventeen

I needed someone to talk to, so I swam over to Shyanna's cave, but she wasn't there. I swam back to Cassie's next, but she was gone too.

I sighed. It didn't really matter. After all, it was Cora I needed to talk to. How would I ever last until her punishment ended? School was two whole days away. I needed to know what she'd learned *now*.

Had Cora talked to Owen? Did she know why he was avoiding me? Was he sick? Had I done something to offend him? I worried and fretted and wondered if there was any way he and I could go back to being best friends. My head kept whispering that I should go ask him, but my heart was too afraid to hear his answer. The thought of losing him was more than I could bear.

I swam by Walrus Waterpark and saw some merkids from merschool, but I couldn't talk to them about my problem. None of them understood how important my friendship with Owen was. No one in Neptunia knew me like Shyanna and Cora.

Finally I swam back to my cave, hoping my dad would be home and could help me figure things out. I swam into the kitchen and saw a note waiting on the counter: "Hi, Rachel. The Queen has asked for an extra private lesson for her sister who's visiting. I'll be home a little late."

I was too distracted to eat, so I swam to my room and stretched out on the bed. I closed my eyes, but all I could see was Owen turning away from me. My heart felt empty. I missed being his friend so much.

Suddenly, out of nowhere, a voice whispered, "Rachel?"

My eyes popped open, and I flipped around in a circle. "Hello?" I called into the water. "Who's there?" My heart was hammering in my chest.

A flash of purple streaked past me into my room. I screamed in shock as a hand reached out and grabbed mine.

"Rachel, it's me," Cora said. She flipped around, moving so quickly she created a wake of water in my room.

"Cora?" I yelled, feeling angry that she'd scared me and embarrassed that I hadn't recognized her voice. "What are you doing here? I thought you couldn't leave your house. Did you sneak out? Oh my gosh, you're going to be in trouble."

"No," Cora said, "but I am in a hurry." She finally stopped spinning and moving. "Mom told me I could swim over as fast as I could when I told her how important this was."

"What?" I cried. "What's wrong?"

"She wouldn't even let me use my shell phone," Cora continued. "'You have five minutes to go to Rachel's and get back home,' she told me."

My heart thumped like a sea otter's tail on the ocean floor. "What?" I cried. "What is it?"

"I don't have long. I have to swim straight home," Cora said.

I grabbed her arm, worried my head would explode if she didn't tell me soon. "Cora! Tell me!"

She put her hand on top of mine. "I know what's wrong with Owen."

My stomach dropped like a bird diving for fish.

"He isn't mad at you at all," Cora said.

"He's not?" I said, feeling a brief moment of relief.

Cora shook her head, and her hair shimmered and flowed in the water.

"Then what is it?" I demanded. "What's wrong?"

Cora finally stopped moving around and froze, staring right at me. "He's moving."

Chapter Eighteen

"He's what?" I said, but it wasn't really a question.

Cora dropped her gaze. She glanced around my room, pretending to be fascinated by the posters of the King and Queen on my cave wall. "Moving. You know, like when you moved to Neptunia from Caspian. But humans have to pack up all their things and rent trucks and drive for hours. It takes so much longer to get around on land."

"I know what moving is," I said quietly. "But where is Owen going? It's not far, right?"

Cora's bottom lip popped out, and she shook her head. "Justin told me it's not good, Rachel. Not good at all. Owen's dad got offered a new job — a good one."

I closed my eyes, preparing for the worst.

"I guess his dad is pretty sure they're going to go," Cora continued. "He's making his final decision soon. Justin said Owen refuses to talk about it with them."

All of a sudden things made sense to me. Why Owen was avoiding me. Why he wouldn't talk to me. We were so close that he knew he couldn't hide his real feelings from me. If he was trying to avoid how he felt, of course he'd have to avoid me too. He didn't hate me!

"I have to go talk to Owen!" I exclaimed.

Cora nodded. "Yeah, you do." She reached out and squeezed my hand. "I'm sorry, Rachel, but I have to go. If I don't get home, I'll never be allowed to leave my cave again!" She hugged me quickly and swam off.

I wanted to go to shore right away, but to avoid getting in trouble, I waited for my dad to come home so I could ask permission. I regretted it, because Dad made me wait until morning. He didn't want me swimming off in the darkness. I knew he was right, but it was still torture. I barely slept a wink that night thinking about Owen moving away.

The next morning, Dad made me eat one of his mussel muffins, and then he swam with me to the exit of the castle on his way to go see Queen Kenna's sister again.

"Be careful, Rachel," Dad said as he swam away. "I'll see you at home tonight."

I nodded and took off. I swam so quickly that my fins were sore by the time I reached shore. I got my legs and ran as fast as they'd carry me up the beach and toward Owen's house. When I reached his front door, my lungs were almost bursting, working overtime breathing in oxygen from air instead of water.

His mom opened the door right away when I knocked, and as soon as she saw me, her eyes filled with tears. “Oh, Rachel,” she said. “Owen’s so upset. He’s going to miss you so much.”

“Then you really are moving?” I said. “For sure?”

Owen’s mom nodded and stepped forward to hug me, resting her chin on top of my head. “You always smell so wonderful,” she said, “almost like the ocean.”

Owen’s parents didn’t know I was half-mermaid or that Owen had special merboy status. They had no clue he could visit Neptunia and swim in the ocean with his temporary merman tail the King and Queen of Neptunia had granted him. Telling them was forbidden.

I glanced up and saw Owen watching from the hallway. His face scrunched up into a frown, but I knew now he wasn’t mad at me.

His mom let me go and turned to see him watching us. She squeezed my hand. “You two need to go take a walk on the beach and talk.”

Owen nodded his head toward the door, and I followed him outside, holding my breath. It was weird the way the air tightened up my lungs. Breathing in water was so much easier.

"I've been so worried about you, Owen," I finally said after we'd walked down the grass toward the pebbled path that led to the beach.

"I know, and I'm so sorry, Rachel," Owen replied. "I've been a jerk." He paused and glanced at me. "I've been so mad. Not at you, obviously, but I couldn't tell you what was going on because I didn't want it to be real. I've been worried too. About leaving Platypus Island. My friends. I didn't want to face any of it."

Owen sighed so loudly I wondered if the mergirls could hear him in the ocean. "But the very worst part is leaving you. I guess I hoped if I didn't talk about it, if I pretended nothing was happening, it would all go away." He stopped and stared at me. "Can you ever forgive me?"

"Oh, Owen, of course!" I told him.

He bit his lip hard, as if trying not to cry. I didn't bother. Tears flowed down my cheeks, and I didn't even feel bad about wasting the mermaid magic in them. The King and Queen didn't like when we shed tears without collecting them, but I couldn't help it. I had no energy to look around for a shell to hold them. Owen's news was the worst. I wanted to grab his hand, pull him to the ocean, and make him stay a merboy forever, never to return to the land again.

"Come on," Owen said, pulling me farther down the beach.

We walked quickly and quietly, as if we could escape our problems by walking away from them. Owen stared up at some lovely yellow birds, shielding his eyes from the bright sun that beamed down, warming my skin. The birds chirped happily, and their wings gliding through the air reminded me of mermaids flipping through the water. The sun felt so hot on land. I had to adjust every time I came to shore.

"So, where are you moving?" I finally asked after we'd walked for a while. I slowed down, ready to face reality, but hoping he'd say his parents had at least decided to move somewhere close to the ocean.

Owen stopped walking, dropped his chin to his chest, and stared down at the flip-flops on his feet. "Montana."

I couldn't help it — I gasped. We'd been studying the geography of land in school, so I knew where he meant. "Montana? As in hundreds of miles away from the ocean?"

Owen nodded. "But that's not even the worst part."

Oh, no! I thought. *What could possibly be worse?*

"We're leaving in two days."

My breath stopped again, and I swallowed. "But that's so soon," I whispered. How could his family go so quickly? Owen and I were finally making up, and now we hardly had any time left to spend together.

Owen nodded. "Once my dad decided, they wanted him to start his new job right away." We both watched a seagull swoop down and steal something from the beach. "My dad says Montana is nice. No other state has as many species of mammals."

I wanted to shout at him that the ocean was much better, but I knew that would only make him feel worse. "Montana looked pretty in the pictures I saw at merschool," I said, trying to be happy for him.

"My dad says I can play on an ice hockey team," Owen added. "It's not the ocean, and it's frozen, but at least it's water. Right?" He bumped my shoulder with his, trying to make a joke.

I tried to smile.

"But the truth is, I'm going to miss the ocean," Owen continued. "And my friends." He glanced sideways. "But most of all you, Rachel. You're my best friend in the whole ocean. In the whole world!"

I looked away and fought back more tears. Owen was my best friend too. I couldn't imagine life without him.

Owen reached for my hand, and we walked like that for a minute. "Will I forget about you?" he asked quietly.

I swallowed a lump. "Yes," I whispered. "If you go too long without being in the ocean, without using your tail . . . the magic will fade. You'll forget all about being a merboy. You'll forget all about my life in the ocean. You might even forget all about me."

My insides felt like I'd been outside in the sun too long with my tail. Dried up and uncomfortable. I was so miserable I wanted to curl up in a ball and cry and cry.

"This is just so sad," I said. "Can you come to the ocean, Owen? Now? To see everyone and everything one more time?"

I needed him to come. I had to convince him to stay. It didn't have to be goodbye. He could come see all the beauty and stay. Owen loved splashing in the ocean with his gorgeous merboy tail. He loved to play with all the ocean creatures. He was as amazing as a merboy as he was as a human. Maybe even more!

Owen glanced back at his house. From where we stood, it looked so tiny and far away. I imagined him swimming away with me and never coming back. We'd take good care of him in the ocean. He could live in our cave. We had extra room.

"I have to text my mom," Owen said. He pulled out his phone, so different than my shell phone. "She'll worry if I'm gone too long. I'll tell her I'm going to your house."

I tried not to think about Owen's mom worrying about him or how she'd feel if he never came back. I had to convince him to stay. That was all that mattered.

Chapter Nineteen

We ran to the water, and Owen slid off his shoes, placing his phone on them and hiding everything in the bushes. As we dove into the ocean, Owen laughed as his beautiful red tail flipped out. I raced in front of him, diving into a wave, and he followed me, whooping as we passed a grumpy-looking walrus.

"It's so beautiful here," Owen said as we swam past schools of brilliantly colored fish and colored coral swaying in the water.

"It is," I agreed. "Maybe you could stay here. You know . . . forever?"

Owen didn't answer. Instead, he swam in circles and laughed with the dolphins as they nosed up beside him. We raced to Neptunia, and when we reached the castle, we spotted Shyanna at the park. She saw us too and a big smile warmed up her beautiful face.

"Owen!" Shy cried happily. She swam close and clapped her hands together. "I'm so glad to see you here. See, Rachel, I knew you two would make up. You're best friends!"

Just like that, my happiness bubble popped. All the sadness I'd been trying to hold in burst to the surface.

"But it's terrible!" I exclaimed. "Everything is horrible!" I managed to hold in my tears knowing the Queen was close by.

"Rachel?" Shyanna patted my back and stroked my hair. She gave Owen a dirty look. "Owen, what did you do to Rachel?"

I shook my head and touched Owen's arm as his happy mood faded too. "No," I told Shyanna. "It's not

Owen's fault. It's just that his family is moving far away — to Montana. Away from the ocean."

Owen quickly explained about his dad getting a new job and how they'd be moving to Montana in two days. Shyanna's shoulders drooped, and she glanced at me with the kind of understanding a good friend has when someone she loves is hurting.

"You could live here!" I burst out. "You love being a merboy! You'd love merschool. You could spend as much time with the sea creatures as you want. And you could still do sports. Everything would be perfect! Stay, Owen. Stay with us!"

Owen's face and tail drooped, and I knew then that it was wrong to ask him that. My selfish bubble was burst.

"I'm sorry," I said. I remembered how my dad had felt when I'd wanted to leave the ocean to become human. Owen would miss his family. They would never know what had happened to him. He'd never be able to go to shore again. He'd miss his legs and being human.

"Let's not be upset," I said, forcing myself to think of Owen. "Let's make sure your last visit to the ocean is fun — not sad and mopey. Let's go see Cora. She can't leave her cave, because she was late coming from shore and worried her family. But her mom will let you in to say goodbye."

We swam off, and I tried to focus on being happy and enjoying the sea life around us. Even if Owen forgot his time with us when he'd been on land too long, I'd never forget him. He was my best friend — in the ocean or out of it.

Cora's mom made an exception because of the circumstances and let her play in her yard with us, so we chased her sisters and laughed with Owen. Before long, though, Owen glanced at me. "I should get back to shore," he told me. "I have a ton to do before we move."

I nodded as he hugged Cora and her sisters.

"Do you want me to come with you?" Shyanna asked, but I shook my head. She nodded, understanding that I needed to have my last moments with Owen alone.

Owen and I swam slowly and more quietly on our way back to shore than we had on the way to Neptunia. When we got close to shore I stopped. “I can’t come all the way,” I said, biting my lip and trying not to cry again. “Let’s say goodbye here.”

Owen nodded. “Thank you,” he said softly. “For being the best friend I ever had. And giving me the best adventures. I’ll never forget you, Rachel. No matter what. I may forget about your tail and the ocean. But I’ll never forget you.”

I smiled and bit my lip even harder, not trusting myself to say anything. Owen swam close and hugged me, then lightly kissed my cheek.

“Let's not say goodbye, let's say see you soon,” he said. And with that, he swam away.

I watched as Owen reached shore, and his tail transformed back into legs. Then he grabbed his shoes and walked up the beach. He turned, staring back out at the water, but I dove down, flipping my tail on the water’s surface to say goodbye.

Chapter Twenty

The rest of the weekend dragged on. I spent most of my time alone in my room, thinking about Owen. On Monday when I swam to school, Cora and Shyanna swam to meet me and gave me big hugs.

"Losing Owen is hard," Cora said. "But you always have us. Friends until the end." She held out her hand, and I laid my hand on top. Shyanna laid her hand on top of mine.

"I made a wish last night," Shyanna told me. "I wished with all the mermaid magic I could muster.

I even looked through the Mermaid Magic Book of Cures."

"But we're not curing anything," I said.

"Maybe we are," she said mysteriously. My friends distracted me with chatter, but I still had a hole in my heart. I managed to drag myself through the school day, and then Shyanna and Cora swam home with me.

Dad was waiting in front of the cave. Someone treaded in the water beside him. Someone who looked an awful lot like Owen!

I squealed and swam forward. "Owen?" I cried. "What are you doing here?"

"He wanted to tell you in person," my dad said with a smile.

"Tell me what?" I asked, trying not to get my hopes up.

"I'm still moving, Rachel," Owen said. "But I snuck back to Neptuna this morning while my parents were packing. I figured it couldn't hurt to ask, so I talked to the King and Queen. I told them I was moving and wouldn't be near the ocean but that I'd be back someday. That I had to come back. I told them I loved Mermaid Kingdom and didn't want to ever forget my time here or being a merboy. I promised never to tell a human what I know. No matter what."

I held my breath in the water.

"And?" Shyanna practically screamed at him.

"And I won't forget!" Owen exclaimed. "I can come back someday. I won't lose my tail."

"They're not taking away your tail?" Shyanna asked. She flipped in a circle. "I knew it! A cure for a broken heart — that's what I wished for! I love mermaid magic!" She was so enthusiastic, we all laughed.

Cora swam closer to Owen. "This means we can stay in touch the way humans do! Justin told me about this thing called the Internet. You can see each other when you talk, even from long distances!"

Shyanna and I giggled, and Owen and my dad grinned. Cora glanced around and her cheeks turned bright pink. "What?" she asked.

"When did you talk to Justin?" Shyanna demanded.

"I, uh, kind of missed him this weekend," Cora said. "And I had a shell I wanted to give him, so I swam to shore before school."

Owen rescued her. "It's true. We really can use the Internet to talk. It won't be the same, but it's better than nothing. You can get the guys to help you." He glanced at Cora then and winked. "I'm sure Justin will be happy to help you girls stay in touch."

We all laughed at the uncomfortable look on Cora's face.

Owen turned back to me. "I have to get home. We're leaving tonight, and I have a lot to do. I told my mom I wouldn't be gone long. But I wanted to tell you I won't forget you. As long as I never tell another human about merlife, I won't have to forget anything!"

"Just like you promised," I whispered.

The mergirls and my dad all grinned, and then it was my turn to blush.

"Come on," I said to my friends. I couldn't wipe the grin off my face.

Shyanna and Cora joined hands, and Owen grabbed mine as we all swam off together. Dad watched from the front of our cave, smiling and waving goodbye.

When we got closer to shore, Shyanna and Cora hung back a little, and I swam slowly with Owen into the shallow water. It was sad saying goodbye again, but knowing we would never forget each other made a big difference.

Owen turned to me and grinned. "I'll come back when I can," he said. "I promise, I'll be back."

"I know," I told him, my insides dancing happily. We hugged each other so tightly I couldn't breathe.

Owen let go first. "I'll see you on the Internet. I'll be in Montana and ready to talk in one week."

“You bet you will,” I told him, excited to learn how the Internet worked.

Owen swam away quickly but turned back before his legs appeared. “I’ll miss you, Rachel Marlin!” he called. “You’re a great best friend.”

“I’ll miss you too!” I called back.

Shyanna and Cora swam to me then, and we watched Owen climb out of the water, off to his new adventures in Montana with his sturdy earth legs.

My friends each grabbed one of my hands, and we swam off together, back to our home in the ocean. I knew we’d see Owen again.

Part Three: Cora's Tale

Chapter Twenty-One

Deep below the waves, in the heart of Neptunia, my cave vibrated with the sounds of mermaid laughter and merboy cheers.

"Wow, Cora," Rachel, one of my best friends, said as she swam up beside me in the kitchen. "I had no idea this party was going to be so . . ."

"Amazing?" I filled in for her as I topped off a bowl of salty seaweed. I grinned.

"Loud," Rachel finished, her eyes open wide as she glanced out at all the merkids gathered in my cave. I'd invited my entire swim team and all of their friends to come celebrate the swim meet next week. It was biggest meet of the season and a huge deal for all the castles. Our team deserved this pre-tournament tradition. Even merkids from other castles and swim teams had shown up.

Shyanna, my other best friend, swam up to my other side and linked arms with me. "*So* loud," she agreed. "But Cora wouldn't want a party any other way!" She winked.

I couldn't help but laugh. Rachel and Shyanna both had small families and weren't used to constant chaos. I, on the other hand, came from a big family. My friends knew I loved parties and being surrounded by people — the fact that today's crowd included merkids from the swim team made me even happier. It was like being part of the Spirit Squad 2 — magical as a morning seahorse dance!

"It's true!" I agreed. I swirled around the water, unable to contain my joy and excitement. Food, fun, and frolicking! My family loved loud celebrations too, and my mom happily darted around, helping with the party, while my dad kept my sisters busy.

The only thing that put a damper on the party was when Regina Merrick, a member of the Spirit Squad, showed up. I still hadn't forgiven Regina for how cruelly she'd treated Rachel in the past, just because Rachel was half-human. Not even forming our own team — Spirit Squad 2 — made Regina's behavior acceptable.

"Don't worry about her," Rachel said when Regina swam into the cave. Regina stuck her nose in the air and swam past, quickly attaching herself to the side of a cute Titania merboy.

I frowned, but Rachel shook her head and said, "Just ignore her." I guess Rachel is better at forgiveness than I am.

Shyanna grabbed a piece of the seaweed from the bowl I was still holding and stuck the long strand into her mouth. "Yum! Such good seaweed!"

We all swam back into the chaos, and I placed the refilled bowl on a seashell table. A few moments later, a group of merboys swooped in and emptied it. They disappeared as quickly as they'd appeared — all except for one. It was the same merboy Regina had attached herself to when she arrived. She was gone now, and he treaded water alone. He smiled at the three of us, his eyes lingering a little longer on Shyanna. I covered my smile with my hand. There was a big grain of salty seaweed lodged in his teeth.

"So I hear your relay team is going to give our team a good race," the merboy said to me, swimming closer. He didn't stop smiling at Shyanna with that big piece of seaweed stuck in his tooth.

Shyanna kindly pointed at her teeth and then at his. The merboy's cheeks turned bright red, and he turned away and dug his finger in his mouth to remove the snack.

Just then, I heard my name being called and turned to see the other members of my relay team.

"Cora!" Jada called again. She waved me over to where she and the rest of my teammates were starting to dance. I thought about joining them, but I noticed Rachel cringing a little. I knew the chaos overwhelmed her a little.

"Go ahead without me!" I called back. I watched as the relay girls chased each other around in a figure-eight dance. Their mermaid tails swished and flashed like a sea rainbow. I clapped my hands and whistled.

"They look as comfortable and carefree with each other as a pod of dolphins," Shyanna said.

"Wow! That's a real compliment! Shyanna, you love dolphins more than merpeople," Rachel teased.

"She does?" the merboy, who was still standing behind us, asked.

"Not entirely," Shyanna said, winking at him.

I glanced back at the merboy. He looked away quickly and licked his salty fingers. He seemed about to say something, but then stopped and turned away, swimming slowly back to the other side of the room.

"There's something suspicious about the way he's skulking around," I muttered.

"Oh, I don't think he's skulking. He seemed nice enough. He's probably just shy or something," Shyanna said.

I didn't necessarily agree, but Rachel grabbed my hand and turned her full-on attention to me. "So are pre-competition parties supposed to help with your big swim meet?"

"Pre-game rituals are important," I told her, quickly forgetting about the merboy. My stomach started dancing, the nerves in my stomach swirling in frenzied circles as I thought about the upcoming swim meet.

"Are you nervous?" Rachel asked.

"You know when you're so excited about something it's all you can think about?" I asked.

Rachel's head bobbed up and down, and Shyanna joined in.

"That's how I feel!"

"You're going to do great!" Shyanna assured me. "Everyone says your relay team is going to win the thirteen-year-old race!"

"Who's on your team?" Rachel asked. She was new to our castle in Neptunia and still learning who everyone was.

"Jada Cotnam, Kaitlyn Lumby, and Cassie Shores." I pointed to Kaitlyn and Jada, who were laughing near the makeshift dance floor.

"Oh, yeah," Rachel said. "I knew. I just couldn't remember." She turned back to me. "You're all such amazing swimmers. And you have a good chance at winning the trophy for the butterfly race."

"Well, I have a chance," I replied. "Shelby Stewart is big competition. She's really fast! And Jada is too."

"Is it weird that you swim on the same team and do relay events together but race against each other in individual races?" Rachel asked.

I shrugged. I didn't want to say it out loud, but it *was* a little strange. I was really competitive and wanted to beat everyone, including the mergirls on my own team, but good sportsmanship was important too. It was important to learn how to compete and stay friends, no matter who won.

"Two-tale races!" someone shouted.

I looked over and saw Jada and Kaitlyn linking their fins together for a two-tail race against Shelby and another mergirl from her castle. Cassie was helping them tie their tails together.

"Take those two-tail races out of this cave!" my mom called as she swam by the merkids getting ready to race.

"Of course," Jada and Kaitlyn replied, swimming toward the exit of the cave. "Those girls are going to need extra room to try and catch up to us anyhow."

Everyone laughed, and most of the merboys and mergirls at the party swam out of the cave to watch the races. Rachel, Shyanna, and I followed.

The two teams lined up. Both pairs had their fins securely tied together for the race. A merboy I didn't know shouted, "Go!" and then Jada and Kaitlyn took off. Shelby and her partner were right beside them.

Almost immediately there was a horrible, screeching cry. Jada and Kaitlyn both stopped, and each girl grabbed at her tail.

"Oh my gosh!" I cried. "There's been an accident!" An accident involving two of my relay team members! I raced toward them, hoping they weren't injured badly. Both mergirls sat on the bottom of the ocean, wearing matching pained looks on their faces.

This seemed like a bad omen of things to come.

And I didn't like bad omens. Not at all.

Chapter Twenty-Two

Someone called the castle merdoctor, and he swam over as fast as he could. The party atmosphere died out quickly when he arrived. Most of the guests left, but the swim team stuck around, waiting for the results. Coach Cara arrived and sat with the girls as the doctor examined their tails. When she swam over to give us the news, I knew it wasn't good. Shyanna and Rachel were on either side of me and each reached for my hand. They knew how much the upcoming swim meet meant to me.

"Kaitlyn and Jada have torn their tails and won't be able to swim in the competition," Coach Cara announced. “They have to rest their fins for at least two weeks.” Everyone groaned. “It’s bad news for all of us,” she continued. “If we don’t compete in the thirteen-year-old relay, we won’t qualify to win the Team Banner. It’s too late to scratch from the event.”

I tried to fight back tears. We all wanted that banner so much. We’d all been busting our tails training. “What happened?” I asked.

“They found a fishing hook in the rope,” Coach Cara said. “It dug into their tails when they started racing. We can’t figure out how the hook got there.”

“This is terrible news!” Cassie said.

Suddenly I had a thought. “What about emergency substitutes?” I looked at my two best friends. “If Rachel and Shyanna swim in the relay, we’ll still have a chance at the banner! Even though they don’t race, they’re registered members of the swim club.”

My two best friends had registered as members of the swim club to support me more than anything else. They practiced with us occasionally, but they didn’t love it like I did, and they never raced. Shyanna and Rachel both preferred singing and performing.

"That could work," Coach Cara replied. "But it's up to Rachel and Shyanna."

"Please, Rachel. Please, Shyanna!" I begged. "We really need you!"

The rest of the swim team echoed my pleas, begging Shyanna and Rachel to swim. Rachel and Shyanna stared at each other, their eyebrows twisted up and a matching frown on their lips.

"I'm not very fast," Shyanna said.

"Me either," Rachel added.

"You might surprise yourselves when you start racing," I told them, "but either way, it doesn't matter. We just need to enter a relay team. We'd be so grateful." I swallowed my own teeny bit of guilt for putting them on the spot, but the truth was we really needed them.

Rachel and Shyanna exchanged another look, and then Shyanna shrugged her shoulders and sighed. "Okay. I mean, if it will help, I'll do it if Rachel will."

Rachel's long, red hair waved in the water as she nodded. "Of course. I'm just worried we'll make your relay team come in last place!"

"Last place is still a place!" I told them, hugging each of them. "Thank you so much! You're helping the whole team."

We all decided to go to the swim track at school and show the girls how to use the starting blocks and how a relay event worked. When we got there, Rachel and Shyanna worked on starts and flip turns, and the rest of us helped them.

After an hour or so, Coach Cara called an end to the impromptu practice. She had to leave but told everyone to stretch and cool off. I swam over to Rachel and Shyanna's lane, where they were both panting.

"Great job!" I told them.

A few minutes later, Cassie and the swimmers gathered around. Cassie gave me a pointed look, and I nodded. "They're ready," I said, looking at my two best friends. "They can be trusted."

Rachel and Shyanna frowned and looked at me with questioning eyes.

"We have something important to show you," Cassie said. "It's an old and very important ritual that's been passed down through generations of racers in Neptune. It's important that you follow our lead, watch what we do, and do exactly the same thing before you race."

The rest of the team nodded solemnly and filed out, swimming in a single line. I waited for Rachel and Shyanna to join the line and swam behind them.

"It's serious, okay?" I whispered to them. "Do you promise to do what we do?"

Rachel and Shyanna turned and stared at me.

"Don't worry," I told them. "It doesn't hurt. But don't underestimate the importance."

Cassie led the procession of racers toward the entrance to our school swim track. I swam up beside my friends. "We're going to be rubbing the Sea Lion's belly. It's a crucial part of competitive racing," I said.

Rachel and Shyanna nodded. They seemed to be taking it seriously as they followed the swim team to the exit of the swimming track cave.

Suddenly a shocked cry rang from the front of the line. A domino cry traveled all the way to the back where Rachel, Shyanna, and I were treading. I sprinted to the front. Cassie's mouth bulged open as wide as the eyes on a pop-eyed goldfish.

I looked where she was staring and gasped. The Sea Lion statue was gone! The only time it moved was when we transported it to swim meets. But now there were only a few greasy fingerprints around the empty space and little piles of sea salt.

I glanced around, panic building, and then burst into tears. Without our good luck mascot, we were doomed. "We'll never win without rubbing the Sea Lion's belly!" I cried. "Someone stole our mascot to destroy our chance to win the Castle Cup!"

And there was no way I would swim my best without it!

Chapter Twenty-Three

Everyone stared at the empty space, shocked into silence. There had to be a reasonable explanation for the Sea Lion to be missing.

I looked around, expecting someone to start giggling and admit they were pulling a grand prank. I waited and waited, but no one fessed up. Finally I swam closer to the empty space. "Hmmm . . . looks like someone left behind traces of salt."

Cassie swam closer too. "It looks like the pink sea salt from Titania Castle!" Titania was home to one of our top swim team rivals.

"Is someone playing a joke? Is this a class prank?" I demanded. "We need to find the Sea Lion before the swim meet. I need to rub that belly!"

Shyanna and Rachel patted my back, trying to sooth me. I tried to take a deep breath, but it was like I'd gulped back a huge dose of krill medicine and it got stuck in my throat.

"We have to find Coach Cara and tell her what's happened!" Cassie said. "She mentioned earlier that she was going to Walrus Waterpark. Come on."

The group took off, swimming so quickly that we created a wake in the ocean.

"Who would do this?" I asked Shyanna and Rachel as we swam toward the park.

My friends shrugged, too out of breath to answer.

"It had to be a rival team," I said. "And it looked like Titania salt where the statue used to be . . ."

At the front of the group, Cassie turned around. "We can't accuse anyone without evidence," she reminded me.

Finlay, one of the fastest merboys on our team, swam up beside me. "Well, we have to get the statue back, or we'll all lose our races!" he said.

We reached Walrus Waterpark as a group. Coach Cara spotted us and frowned, swimming toward us immediately. "What's wrong?" she asked.

Everyone started talking at once, rushing to get the story out. Finally Coach Cara held up her hands for silence.

"Everyone calm down!" she said. "Rubbing the Sea Lion's belly is a tradition, but it's only a superstition. And superstitions aren't real. It's like believing a black catfish crossing a stream in front of you will bring you bad luck."

"But it *does*!" Finlay said. "My brother had a black catfish cross a stream in front of him once, and he was almost spotted by humans five minutes later."

"Then maybe it was *good* luck," Coach Cara said. "Maybe he *would* have been spotted if the black catfish hadn't been there."

I knew Coach Cara was trying to calm us down, but I also knew in my heart that we needed to get that Sea Lion back. "There were salt and salty smears where the statue used to be!" I told her. "Exactly like the salt the Titania team uses on their seaweed snacks! They have to be the ones who stole the Sea Lion. They're trying to mess up our luck!"

All the merkids started talking at once.

Coach Cara clapped her hands together until we were quiet once again. "I will talk to the Titania coach and see if she knows something. But it could have been anyone. Please," she said glancing at each of us, "don't let this mess with your minds. You don't need the mascot to win the banner."

I was silent, but deep down, I knew she was wrong. I couldn't race until we found out who had taken the Sea Lion — and got it back.

Chapter Twenty-Four

The Titania team denied knowing the whereabouts of our Sea Lion mascot. Their coach asked every member of her team and told Coach Cara that no one knew a thing. Without some kind of proof, there was nothing we could do.

Days went by, and there was still no sign of the Sea Lion. Our swim meet was right around the corner. And yet, my teammates seemed to have forgotten about the importance of our ritual. Or at least none of them seemed as worried as I was. After a while, no one even brought it up.

I was the only swimmer who was having trouble making my times in practice. I knew I was being superstitious, but I couldn't help myself. I believed in my heart that the Sea Lion had to be found. It seemed like it was up to me to solve the mystery.

"Shyanna! Rachel! Great job today!" I called to my friends after practice. They were trying hard to race faster and had improved a lot in a couple of days.

"Thanks," Rachel said with a smile.

"Are you two busy?" I asked. "I was hoping you guys would come with me to Titania. I want to look around their castle. I think we're missing out on an important clue. The salt near the Sea Lion spot had to mean something. There are a couple of swimmers I'd like to talk to. See if I can crack them. Find out more."

Rachel and Shyanna glanced at each other and then back at me. "We made plans to go to shore," Rachel said. "We didn't ask you because we thought

you were babysitting. Justin and Morgan want us to help find seashells." At the mention of the human boys we knew onshore, Rachel winked. "Justin seemed disappointed you weren't coming. But now you can! We're going to go on their computer and talk to Owen."

I was a little tempted. Justin *was* cute. But . . . "Wouldn't you rather go to Titania Castle?" I asked. "Shyanna?"

Shyanna shot a look at Rachel. "I'm sorry, Cora, but we promised."

"I haven't gone in a while because we've been so busy training for the swim meet," Rachel added.

"Why don't you come with us instead?" Shyanna pressed. "Have some merfun? Stretch out your legs."

I shook my head, disappointed I couldn't join them, but determined to get to the bottom of things. "I have a hunch I'm onto something," I told them. "I need to go and check it out. It's important. For the whole swim team."

They both tilted their heads and blinked at me, as if they were worried and weren't sure what to say.

"Well, be careful, Cora," Rachel said. "You should take another merperson with you."

I shrugged. "Everyone is busy," I said, even though I hadn't really asked. I didn't want to do this with anyone else other than my best friends.

We swam together toward the exit of the castle and waved at the guards. Outside, I turned left to head for Titania, while Rachel and Shyanna headed the opposite way to go to shore.

As if the sea life sensed my mood, the swim to Titania was quiet. No dolphins swam over to entice me to play. No crabs or lobsters waved along the way. I caught sight of a few old eels, but they just watched me with their big eyes and didn't greet me at all.

When I finally reached Titania, I swam into the entrance and nodded at the guard who was stationed there. "I'm here to visit a friend from the swim team," I told him with a fake smile. When he nodded,

I quickly swam past before he could ask any other questions.

Once inside, I made my way around the castle grounds. The layout was similar to Neptunia, so I knew where to find caves and parks. I peered into places where a merperson might be able to hide a Sea Lion mascot, but I didn't see anything.

When I swam close to the water park, I spotted a group of merboys goofing around. I swam behind them, hanging back as they swam to a smaller park. They joined a group of mergirls on swings. I watched, missing Shyanna and Rachel and thinking of them on the shore with the human boys.

Maybe I should have gone with them, I thought briefly. I shook my head. *No. I need to solve this mystery.*

I swam closer to the group, listening and looking for anything that seemed unusual. No one seemed suspicious. No one talked in hushed tones about the upcoming swim meet or the missing Sea Lion.

After a moment, I spotted a familiar-looking merboy swimming off by himself a little. He seemed to be watching the merkids play, but not taking part, as if he were preoccupied. He held a long strand of salted seaweed taffy in his hand. He chewed on it, getting salt all over his hands and his face.

Suddenly a jellyfish light went off in my head. That was the boy from my cave party! He was the one who'd given me strange vibes with the way he'd been skulking around. He'd disappeared right before we'd gone to the swim track to coach Rachel and Shyanna. Right before we'd discovered the missing Sea Lion! He looked dodgy, as if he could be hiding something — like a mascot from another castle!

I watched as he swam off, leaving little smears and piles of salt around him. I glanced around to see if anyone was watching, then followed behind. I felt it in my tail. This had to be the boy who had stolen the mascot! I didn't know why or how he'd done it, but I was going to find out.

Chapter Twenty-Five

I followed the merboy as he swam away from the park, toward a long line of caves. He stopped suddenly and looked around, and I darted behind a nearby boulder in the nick of time. The merboy kept chewing on the salty snack, and I realized his fingers would likely leave streaks on anything he touched — streaks like the ones we'd seen at the missing statue site.

A sound squeaked near me, and the merboy looked over his shoulder, toward me.

Squeak. Squeak.

A starfish on the ocean floor smiled up at me, and I frowned and shook my head at him. He exaggeratedly frowned back and then squeaked again, as if we were playing a game. What a little slimer! Usually starfish were the quietest creatures in the ocean, but this one wanted to play.

Luckily the merboy didn't seem to care. He turned away from the boulder and looked around before he swam past the caves toward what looked like an undeveloped part of the castle. In a moment, he disappeared into the darkness.

I hesitated for just a moment and then swam after him. Scary-looking fish watched me with their mouths open and their pointy teeth bared. Coral waved in the darkness but instead of looking beautiful, it seemed menacing and scary. I wondered for a moment whether I was doing something really foolish but swallowed that thought and kept going.

The merboy swam up to a tall shape covered by a cloth of seaweed. It looked like the shape of a sea lion! I gasped out loud, and the boy turned, his face evil and menacing in the dark shadows and murky

bubbles. He spotted me staring at him, and his eyes flashed in anger.

"I knew it!" I cried, trying to sound brave. "You stole our Sea Lion statue to jinx our swim team! That is so horrible . . . and . . ." I struggled to think of something else to say. "Mean," I finished, jutting out my chin farther.

The boy glared at me, and I looked around, realizing I was all alone in this dark area of the ocean with a suspicious and possibly dangerous thief. He swam at me so quickly it took my breath away. I did a quick backstroke to put some distance between us.

"What are you talking about?" he asked. His face was bright red, but he looked confused. "And why did you follow me here? You don't even live in this castle. What in the ocean are you up to?"

"Me?" I swam forward. "Don't pretend with me, thief!" I faked sounding brave as I rushed past him and reached for the seaweed cover, yanking it off the statue.

It wasn't the Sea Lion.

Underneath the cover was a tall cabinet with several shelves. Some contained sharp tools like shark teeth and dead coral. On the top were lumps of clay from the ocean floor. I blinked, looking around the darkness. It had to be here.

"Where is it?" I cried. "Where's the Sea Lion?"

The boy swam closer. He didn't look embarrassed anymore. Judging by the squint in his eyes and the stiffness in his tail, he was annoyed. "What are you talking about? Why did you follow me here? What are you doing here skulking around?"

"I'm not the skulker," I said, crossing my arms. But my voice was low as I realized I might have made a big mistake and also made quite a fool of myself.

The merboy crossed his own arms and stared back at me.

"You stole our Sea Lion," I said weakly. "Our team mascot. At least I thought you did."

He shook his head. "No, I didn't. Why in the ocean would I do that?"

My cheeks burned. I glanced around, but there was no Sea Lion hiding anywhere. "I think I was wrong. I might owe you an apology."

The merboy started to laugh then, and a tiny feeling of relief joined the embarrassment and fear already swirling around my merbody.

"No offense, but that's the most ridiculous thing I've heard," he said. "Why would I steal your Sea Lion when I'm planning on cheering for your team?" He glanced around then, a little suspiciously again. "Well, maybe I won't cheer out loud, I don't want to be a traitor to my own castle."

"Why would you cheer for Neptunia?" I asked him.

The boy glanced down at his fins. "Your friend," he said quietly. "Shyanna, the nice one. The pretty one. The one who likes dolphins."

I studied the merboy and realized he wasn't scary or dangerous or suspicious at all. His mouth had salt in the corner, and his ears were the color of a red mussel shell. He had a crush on Shyanna. I covered my smile with my hand. I was such an idiot!

"I made this for her," he continued. He reached over and took a beautifully carved clay dolphin off one of the shelves. The detail was amazing. The eyes looked so real, I almost expected it to click and whistle and swim away.

"You made this?" I practically shouted.

His ears turned bright red again, and I slowly realized the truth about what was going on — he was embarrassed. He was hiding his talent in this dark place like it was a bad thing.

"It's amazing," I told him. "Shyanna will love it. She's crazy about dolphins."

"I know," he said. "I heard, and I wanted to surprise her."

"That's why you were skulking around?" I asked. "To spy on Shyanna?"

"I wasn't skulking or spying," he muttered, but he lowered his eyes.

I smiled. "I'm kidding." He'd been trying to get closer to Shyanna. It was sweet. "I'm sorry. I thought you were . . . never mind. It's beautiful. You're very talented. What's your name?"

"Kai." He looked up. "Do you think she'll like it? She won't think it's . . . weird? I know merkids our age don't exactly think doing clay sculptures is cool. Everyone seems to care more about swim races and winning the Castle Cup Banner."

"Shyanna's very artistic. She's an amazing singer." I stared at him, confused. "But you're on the swim team too, aren't you?"

"I only joined so I could go to your party," he explained. "I'm not racing or in any relays or anything. I knew I had to go to your party when I saw Shyanna in the singing competition."

"Yeah, she's really good. But it seems like you're fast," I added. I had a hard time understanding how any merperson could *not* want to race if he or she were fast.

He shrugged. "I have other interests."

So did Shyanna and Rachel, I realized. Not everyone loved racing like I did. "She'll love it," I said.

Kai had a million questions about Shyanna after that. I answered as many as I could stand before I finally got back to my main reason for being in this castle.

"Do you know who might have stolen the Sea Lion?" I finally asked when I couldn't stand it any longer. I told him about the pile of salt where the Sea Lion statue usually stood, the reason I'd suspected him in the first place.

"Well, everyone in Titania loves salt," Kai said, "but the same can be said for most of the castles in Mermaid Kingdom. And I know for a fact no one from our castle would be able to steal a sea lion and get it past our guards."

"Why not?" Guards were good at keeping secrets. Everyone knew that.

"Because sea lions are considered bad luck by all of Titania," Kai told me.

"Really?"

He nodded. "Really. The king lost one of his merbabies to a sea lion and banned them from our castle years ago."

"Oh." I deflated a little and glanced down at my shell watch. "I have to get back. I'm supposed to babysit my sisters soon."

"Come on then, I'll swim with you to the gates." He started swimming back toward the lighter part of the ocean. I followed. "Don't worry," he added. "I've seen you race. You don't need a mascot to make you faster."

I shook my head and chewed on my bottom lip.

"You're superstitious!" he said. "Are you like mermen who won't shave before water polo championships and grow really long beards?"

I shrugged. "Maybe a little." My heart dragged like a fishing net through the ocean. I still hadn't solved the mystery of the missing Sea Lion mascot.

We swam quietly for a while, and before I knew it, we'd almost reached the castle entrance.

"Can you do me a favor?" Kai asked.

"Sure. Anything." I felt bad for suspecting him of stealing the Sea Lion.

"Don't tell Shyanna I made her the dolphin," he said. "I want to surprise her at the race."

I covered my smile. "Sure," I said.

"I heard Shyanna's on your relay team now," Kai added.

"Yeah, she is."

He grinned. "Good. And good luck in the butterfly race. I know Shelby Stewart, from Hercules Castle, has been telling everyone she's going to win this year. She's done everything she can to beat you. But I know you'll get her."

I stopped for a moment, treading water. That was it! I'd figured out who the real suspect was — Shelby Stewart. I don't know why I hadn't thought of it sooner. She really wanted to win the butterfly race. Would she go to any lengths to beat me?

I had to find out.

Chapter Twenty-Six

I made a few detours as I swam back to Neptunia, collecting some rare and delicious mussels and shrimp from a place I'd discovered with my friends. I lucked out and also found a spotted dogfish egg capsule. Mermaids used them as purses, and I tucked the rare finds and treasures inside my new bag.

When I got back to Neptunia, I smiled my friendliest smile at the two guards on either side of the entrance. I even batted my eyelashes a little, but they didn't react. All castle guards are well trained and rarely respond to anything with more than a shift in their eyes. But the guards all trained together, which meant they were friendly with each other. It only made sense that the guard at our castle would know a lot about what was going on at the other castles. If only I could find a way to get them to talk.

Fortunately, one of the guards had a son who went to my school. He always talked about how his dad had a weakness for rare fish. He told us about hunts they'd go on, and how his dad always wished he had more time to hunt.

My luck seemed to be improving because the boy's dad was one of the guards on duty.

I stopped just past the entrance. "I have a question," I said out loud, as if I were talking to the coral walls of the castle. I glanced over, and the biggest guard frowned and shook his head. It was against the rules to talk to him if he hadn't spoken first, but I was desperate and acting foolish. I couldn't seem to help myself.

I reached into my newly acquired mermaid purse and took out a big, juicy shrimp, so rare I'd almost fainted with happiness when I'd spotted it lurking under a sea plant. "This is one of the rarest shrimp in the ocean. I can't even believe I found it. I wonder if there's any mermen who could truly appreciate it."

The guard narrowed his eyes. "Miss Bass, guards do not take bribes from merchildren. Guards do not take bribes from *anyone*."

I knew that too, but I also knew that once he'd spoken to me, I was free to talk to him. And despite what he'd said, I noticed he couldn't help staring at the shrimp. "Of course. I would never bribe anyone. I mean, what would a merkid like me even need to bribe a guard for?" I fake laughed. "That's so ridiculous no one would even believe it."

Both of the guards glared at me. I hoped they couldn't tell how badly my hands were shaking or how nervous I was.

"It's just that . . . well . . . I know it might seem silly when you have the important job of protecting our castle, and I'm just a thirteen-year-old merkid,

but our swim team — as you probably know — is swimming in the Castle Cup. I'm on the swim team, and I hate to brag, but I have a pretty good chance of winning a few races. I just love racing so much."

Neither guard looked at me. They both stared straight out, the way they were supposed to. But they didn't tell me to keep quiet or be on my way, so I kept going.

"The thing is, our team mascot, the Sea Lion, went missing — as in someone took it. And it's a silly superstition, but we always rub that Sea Lion's belly before every race. It's good luck."

One of the other guards nodded his head once and grunted. "I was on the swim team. We rubbed his belly for luck. Tradition."

"Yes!" I exclaimed. "So you understand how important this mascot might be?"

Neither answered. I nonchalantly waved around the shrimp. "Mr. Waters, I go to school with your son. I was thinking I might offer him some of my rare fish finds. You know, because he's a friend, and his family is so well respected in our community. It's like a thank you for a job well done. A job that we kind of take for granted. And Mr. Warley, I know your wife is a good friend of my mom's. My mom makes a mean shrimp pie, and I'm going to make sure she gets one to your wife."

They didn't move. "Be careful, Miss Bass," the biggest one said. "You're walking on a fine fish line."

"Oh, I don't mean anything by it," I said quickly. "Just that I know nothing gets by guards. Like, for instance, if someone were to take the Sea Lion out of Neptunia. Say to Hercules Castle, where Shelby Stewart swims. You would know, right?"

The guards actually loosened their stance for a moment. They looked at each other and then back at me. My heart beat faster, hoping they knew something.

But then the big guard shook his head and looked right at me. I saw pity in his eyes. "No one on my staff reported the Sea Lion leaving the castle."

I let out the breath I'd been holding, and my hope dropped to the bottom of my fin.

"And besides, Coach Cara already checked with us. We haven't seen anything resembling the Sea Lion leaving these gates."

"So that means the Sea Lion is still in Neptunia?" I asked.

The guard almost smiled. "I can't say that for sure, but what I *can* say is that it would take a great deal of work and planning to sneak something like the Sea Lion out of the castle. I suspect it would take a lot of trouble — more trouble than some schoolkids pulling a prank would be interested in."

In my heart, I knew they were right. But I also couldn't accept the fact that the Sea Lion was still in Neptunia. Would someone in our own castle want to jeopardize the swim team's chances of winning the Castle Cup? It made no sense. It was easier to believe that Shelby Stewart was much more cunning than I'd ever given her credit for.

I had to find out.

Chapter Twenty-Seven

The next morning, I was so tired from trying to figure out who would have stolen the Sea Lion that my mom had to wake me. Then I had to help get my sisters ready for the day and got behind on my whole schedule.

I raced to the swim track after helping with my sisters, but everyone on the team was already at the pool doing laps in the lanes or stretching out. Rachel and Shyanna were sitting on the edge of the pool, their fins flapping in the water as they timed the thirteen-year-old merboys doing the backstroke.

I smiled when I saw Shyanna, thinking of the dolphin Kai had made her. She would be surprised and probably a little embarrassed but pleased! He was cute and actually seemed very nice. She would probably be kind of thrilled that a merboy like him had a crush on her.

"Hey, Sherlock Mermaid, did you sleep in?" Shyanna called, smiling to show she was joking.

I waved at her and shrugged. I'd already told them on the shell phone about my adventure the day before and that the Titania boy I'd suspected hadn't been the one who'd stolen the Sea Lion. They'd both been shocked when I'd also revealed how I'd spoken to the guards and was giving them rare shrimp as a *reward*.

"Rachel and I are coming over after practice because your mom is going to braid our hair for the swim meet," Shy said when I swam over.

"Okay, good." I dove into a swim lane to do my warm-up and concentrated hard while I swam, trying to get rid of all my angst and worries. But no matter how hard I focused, I felt stiff and a little off. Images of the Sea Lion danced in front of my eyes.

When I looked up from my set, Cassie, Kaitlyn, and Jada were on the side of the pool giving tips to Rachel and Shyanna on their flip turns. "Come on, Cora!" Cassie called. "Let's do a run-through and show these girls how fast they can go."

"Sure." I swam under the lane ropes toward them, and Shyanna and Rachel swam over to the side of the pool. I would be first up on the blocks and first in the water, which meant I had to set the pace. Cassie would go last and bring the team home.

I swam first and was a little off my time, but I was excited to see how fast Rachel and Shyanna could swim their parts of the race. Cassie and I cheered from the sides as they completed their laps. Kaitlyn was flipping in circles, clapping and whooping, but I noticed that Jada had a sour look on her face. I also noticed that she was eating a salty seaweed snack.

Something in my mind clicked. Kaitlyn was always teasing Jada about her salty tooth. Could it be? I didn't want to think one of my teammates could be responsible. My fins felt cold at the possibility.

Shyanna and Rachel were excited after the practice race and almost piled on top of me after we completed our cool-down. I pretended to be as excited as they were, but I couldn't help feeling weird when we swam past the empty spot where the Sea Lion was supposed to be. I seemed to be the only one who noticed, though. Jada, Kaitlyn, and Cassie swam off without giving it a second glance.

Rachel and Shyanna swam with me back to my house. Shyanna was chatting about the human boys and seeing Owen on the computer, the only way he could communicate with us now that his family had moved away. Rachel was a little quieter when his name came up. I could tell she missed seeing her human best friend in person. I was quiet too, thinking about the Sea Lion, wishing I could rub his belly for luck.

When we reached my cave, Mom greeted us and handed each of us a slice of shrimp cake on a shell plate. After we ate, she took us to her room to do our hair. She'd sent my sisters off with my dad to go play with the dolphins at the park and had set out all her favorite shells to braid in. I mostly listened as the girls giggled and chatted with my mom.

Shyanna went first, and her blond hair looked stunning when mom was done. Rachel went next, and her red hair sparkled with pearls. Finally it was my turn. Mom sat me down in her chair and ran a brush through my hair. "This mergirl has been distracted for days," she said to my friends.

Rachel and Shyanna exchanged a look. "Well, she's pretty worried. You know. About the swim meet."

"Oh, I know," my mom said. She separated a thick strand of my hair and started to weave in some shiny pearls. "You know, Cora, rubbing the Sea Lion's belly is just good fun. It's an old tradition."

"No, Mom. It's more than that," I told her as she worked her magic on my hair.

"Only if you believe it is," she said softly.

That was the thing. I *did* believe. And believed I had to find it.

After Mom was done braiding our hair, I swam outside with the girls before they went back home to their own caves. "I had an epiphany at practice today," I told them as we swam to the yard. "About the Sea Lion."

"What in the ocean is an epiphany?" Shyanna asked with a pretend frown.

"You know what an epiphany is," I told her.

She glanced at Rachel and then back at me. "Okay, it's just that . . . well, Cora, we're worried about you."

"No, listen," I said. "It's Jada. She's always eating salty snacks. And she's been acting weird lately. Like she didn't even seem that happy that you're swimming so well."

"Cora, you're obsessed. You're becoming suspicious of everyone," Rachel said with a shake of her head. "Let's not just wonder and gossip about it. If you really want to know, let's go to Jada's and find out. We'll ask her outright instead of talking behind her tail. And then you can see that you're wrong. Remember, Jada tore her fin. Maybe she's upset because she can't race. Let's talk to her and find out what she has to say for herself."

I stared at her for a long moment, then I reached for her and hugged her. "You're right, Rachel. I'm sorry. I am being horrible. Talking about merpeople and suspecting everyone. I should know better. Let's do it. Let's go talk to Jada and ask her."

"Nicely," Rachel added.

"Oh, Cora, what are we going to do with you?" Shyanna said, throwing an arm around me.

I hugged her back. I was so lucky to have them. Shyanna understood competitiveness, and Rachel was thoughtful about everything.

Together we set off for Jada's cave. When we reached it, I glanced around. There were salty fingerprints all over the cave door. Just like the prints at the Sea Lion statue. More proof! I held my breath and swam closer.

Inside the cave, I heard Jada and someone else — it sounded like Kaitlyn — arguing.

"It's not nice!" Kaitlyn was saying.

"I don't care!" Jada replied. "I'm upset. I wish we were the ones racing, not them."

I couldn't contain myself. This was proof! Jada didn't want us racing without her. "I know what you did!" I yelled, bursting into the cave. "You stole the Sea Lion to jinx your own swim team!"

Rachel and Shyanna quickly swam after me, their mouths wide open. "Um, Cora?" Rachel said. "What exactly are you doing?"

I glared at Jada and Kaitlyn, who looked shocked to see me. "Getting to the bottom of this," I said.

"This isn't exactly what I had in mind," Rachel said. "I was picturing something a little more polite."

"What are you talking about?" Jada asked.

"I heard you say that you didn't want us winning."

Jada frowned. "I never said that. I said I wished *we* were racing." She looked at Rachel and Shy. "No offense. You guys are doing great. But it's really hard to watch from the sidelines." She pointed down at the bandaged scar on her fin.

"I know!" Rachel said. "I get that. Of course you wish you could be racing." She turned and glared at me. "It's completely normal to feel that way. We wish you were racing too!"

"But I still want you to win," Jada said. "And I didn't steal the Sea Lion. That's crazy."

"But you're always eating seaweed. There are salty fingerprints everywhere!" I said. "Just like we found near where the statue should be."

Jada burst into tears. I looked at her, completely confused.

"It's because of a boy," Kaitlyn explained. "Kai Joustra. He's from Titania Castle. Jada has the biggest crush on him. He eats that seaweed all the time, so she thought if she ate it too, it might somehow make him like her. But Kai just told her he's got a crush on another mergirl and that he only likes Jada as a friend."

I glanced quickly at Shyanna, but she didn't appear to have any clue that *she* was the mergirl Kai liked. Oh dear, life was complicated sometimes. Rachel hugged Jada close and told her she understood.

I felt terrible. I'd been so focused on my own worries, I'd barely noticed what was going on around me. I didn't feel proud.

I had to change things.

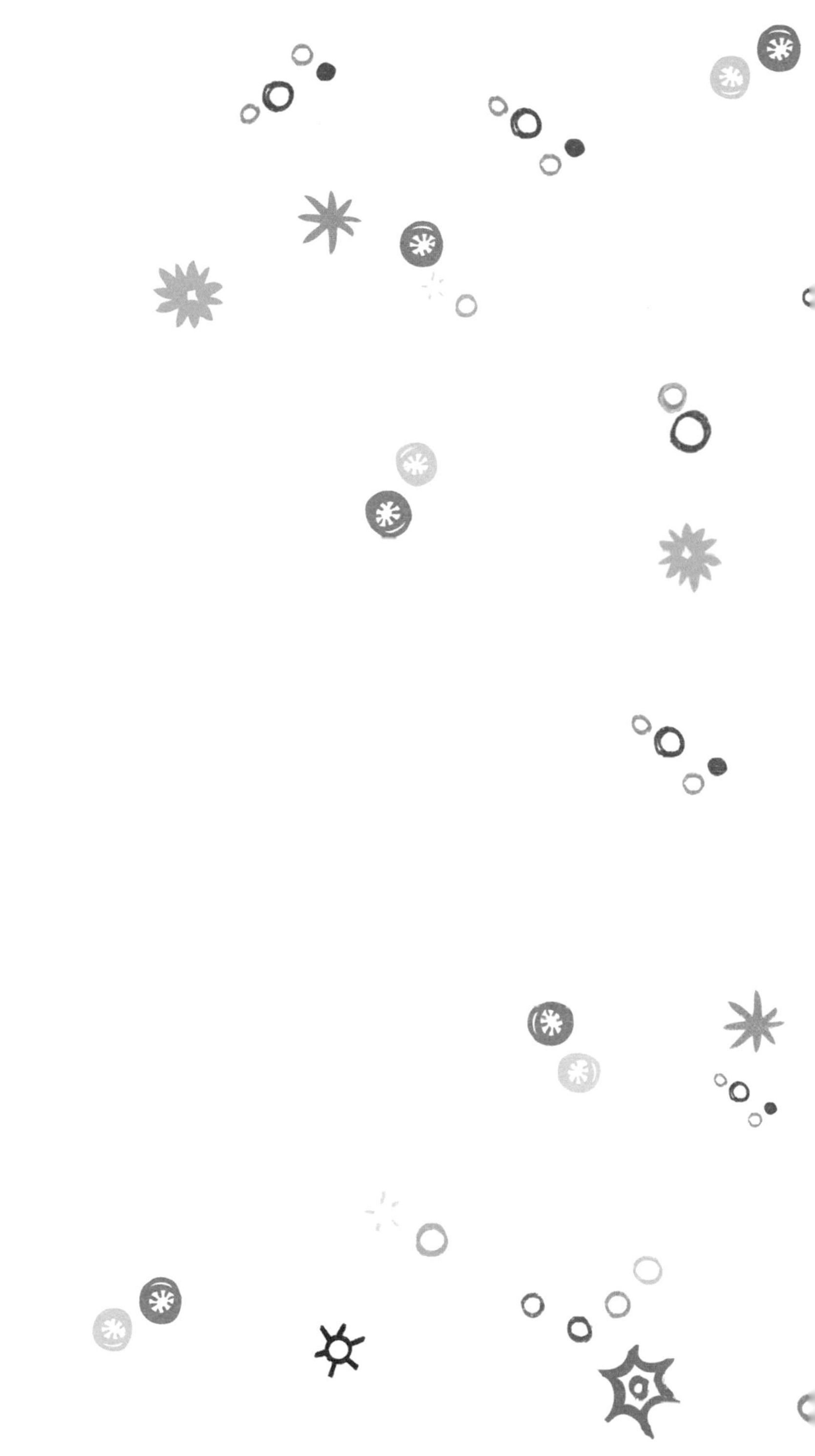

Chapter Twenty-Eight

The day of the big swim meet was almost upon us. One more day to go, and still no sign of the Sea Lion. I'd tried to stop looking for guilty signs everywhere. I told myself it didn't matter whether I rubbed that belly or not. I told myself that winning wasn't as important as trying my best. I reminded myself that I'd become so obsessed and superstitious that I'd lost sight of what was important — my friends.

I tried to put all thoughts of the Sea Lion out of my mind. I tried really hard . . . but I couldn't do it. Because the truth was, someone had taken the Sea Lion. Someone from Neptunia. Someone who didn't want our team to have good luck. And that was something I just couldn't figure out or understand.

I didn't say anything to Jada about Kai's crush on Shyanna. I was beginning to realize that merboys might make sea life more complicated. Maybe that's why I preferred human boys. My cheeks warmed thinking of Justin. He was someone else I needed to go and visit. I hadn't seen him once since the Sea Lion had disappeared. I needed to go to land when this race was over. But the worst thing was, I couldn't even tell him about it. He didn't know I was a mermaid.

"Come on, Cora, kick that tail harder!" Coach Cara shouted at me from the side of the pool lane.

It was our final practice before the big race, and everyone was giving it their all. I didn't use the Sea Lion as an excuse. Instead, I pressed on, working as hard as I could.

Coach Cora clapped when my hands touched the edge of the pool. "You beat your best time!" she yelled.

My friends were on the sidelines watching, and they all cheered loudly. Rachel, Shyanna, Cassie, Kaitlyn, and Jada wiggled their tails and clapped!

"You don't need the Sea Lion!" Jada called.

I smiled and pumped my fist in the air. Maybe I didn't need luck after all. Maybe I could make my best times all on my own.

"You're right!" I shouted to Jada. "I needed you as my teammate, pushing me and making me faster. I'll race this one for both of us!"

Jada smiled, and I could see how much my comment meant to her. It was true. Swimming with Jada had made me faster. I made me faster. Not the Sea Lion.

Coach Cara lined us up for the relay, and we raced against the twelve-year-old girls. They had some fast swimmers, and even though we gave them a good race, they still managed to beat us by a couple of seconds.

"That's amazing!" I said, high-fiving Rachel, Shyanna, and Cassie. "A couple of days ago, they would have beat us by a lot more than a couple of seconds. You guys were amazing."

Rachel and Shyanna had really saved us. They weren't as fast as Jada and Kaitlyn, but they were showing up and doing their best for our team. We couldn't ask for more. The girls headed to the team cave to fix their fancy braids, while I took a little extra time cooling down.

When I swam out of the race lanes and headed for the changing room, I heard a familiar voice — Regina Merrick. She was surrounded by members of her Spirit Squad, and she was laughing. "Did you see how pathetic the thirteen-year-olds swam? They couldn't even beat a bunch of twelve-year-olds. I told you it would happen like this."

I swam inside and saw that Regina had her back to the door. A couple of girls from the Spirit Squad spotted me, but Regina didn't and kept going.

"They're going to make fools of themselves at the Castle Cup," she said. "They're all so superstitious, it's ridiculous. It's a good thing their Spirit Squad isn't performing too. That would be so embarrassing for us. We're the only thing that's going to give our castle any credibility. We are why Neptunia is the envy of all the other castles in the kingdom."

Just then, Regina noticed her friends staring. Then they all looked down, not saying anything. Regina slowly turned her head and saw me standing there.

"Oh, it's you," she said. "Whatever. It's a good thing you wear loser so well." She flicked her long hair and then turned away from me as if I was so unimportant it didn't matter what she said behind my back or in front of my face. "You're going to get a lot of practice at it."

I stared at the back of her head. And in that moment, I knew the truth. Regina was the one who'd taken our mascot.

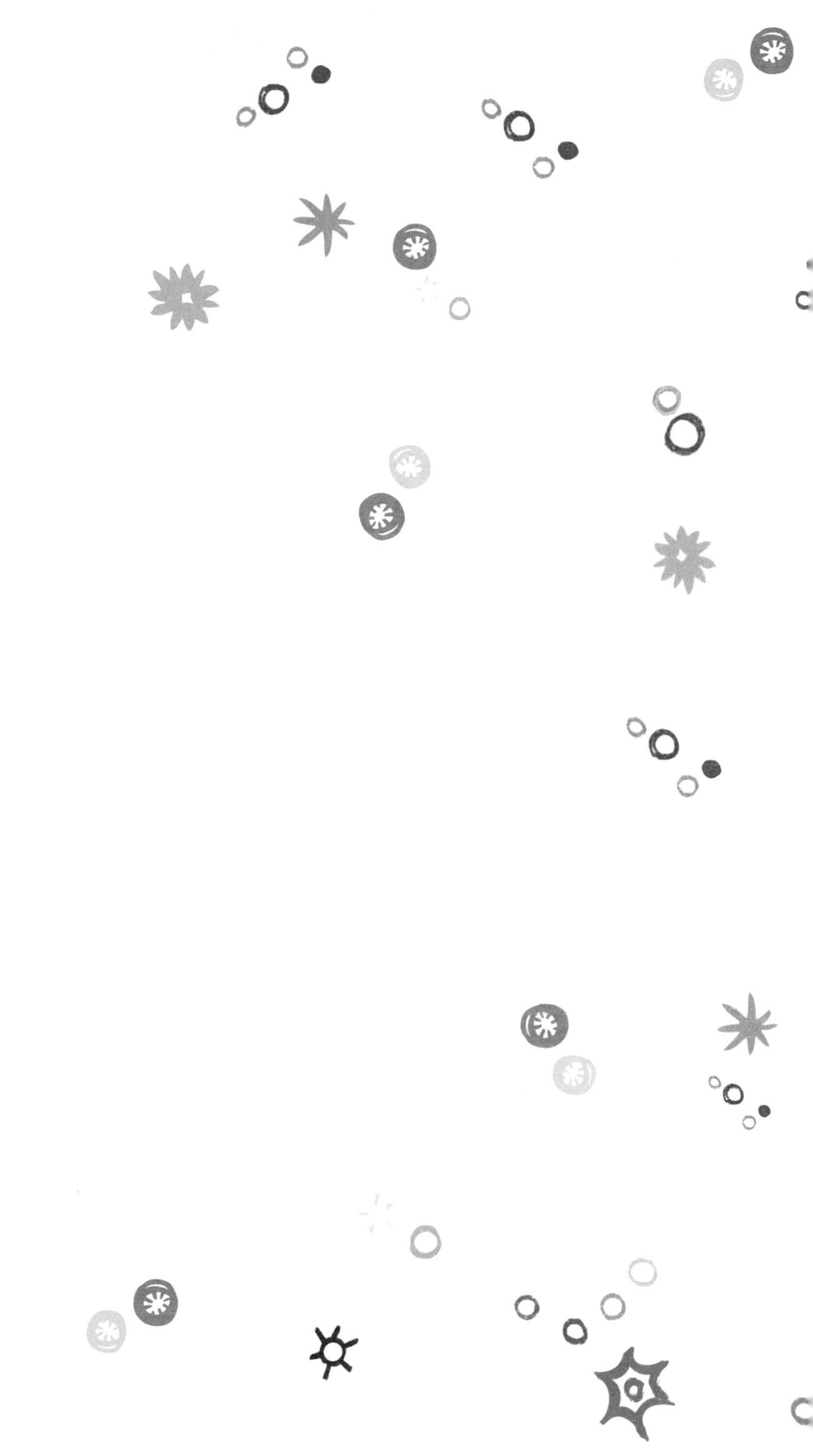

Chapter Twenty-Nine

I swam toward my cave, stopping when I reached my front yard. Shyanna, Rachel, Cassie, Jada, and Kaitlyn were all out front. My little sisters were climbing all over them — and the Sea Lion mascot.

I gasped. "You found it!" I said. "How did you figure out who took it?"

"Regina didn't know we were in the shower while she was talking to you," Rachel told me.

"And the way she was talking about the team made it pretty clear she didn't want us to win,"

Shyanna said. "So we waited until they left, and then we got Rachel's dad and swam to Regina's house. My dad talked to her parents, and we found where she'd hidden the Sea Lion in her cave basement. Her parents had no idea it was there."

"How'd you even get it here?" I asked.

"A couple of guards heard we found it and swam over to help bring it here," Shyanna explained.

"You figured out it was her too, didn't you?" Rachel asked. "How come you came home instead of going to her house?"

"I realized I didn't need it anymore," I said as I swam closer. Then I darted over to the statue and rubbed the belly as hard as I could. "But I'm so glad you got it! You're the best friends in the whole ocean!"

We all laughed and hugged, and my little sisters crawled all over me, demanding I let them rub the belly too.

"The guards offered to bring it to the swim meet tomorrow," Rachel told me. "Under special guard."

I smiled at her. “I don’t think we need it. We make our own luck.”

Rachel swam right at me and hugged me so hard I could barely breathe. “I’m glad you realized that,” she said.

“Thank you, Rachel,” I whispered in her ear. “For going to get it for me.”

“You’d have done the same for me,” she said.

Shyanna hugged the two of us. “We’d do anything for each other!”

Cassie called Coach Cara on her shell phone, and in minutes the whole swim team arrived, cheering when they saw our mascot. We carted the Sea Lion back to its spot at the pool, and everyone agreed to leave the mascot there for this swim meet.

Mystery solved. In the end, it was Regina being Regina. And I had no doubt she’d be dealing with the consequences of her actions.

In the meantime, we had races to swim!

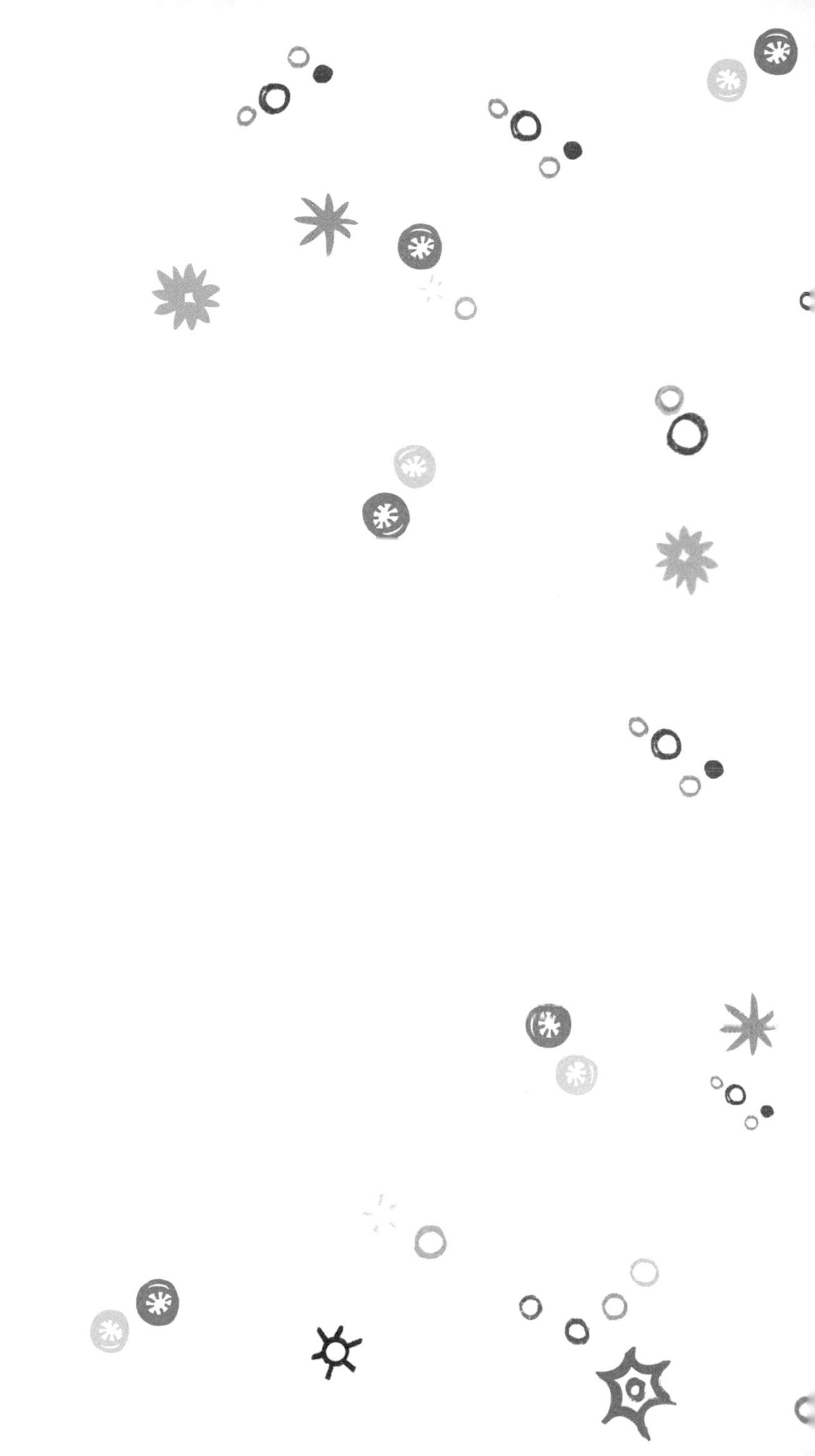

Chapter Thirty

The whole school and most of the castle showed up for the swim meet. Even the King and Queen of Neptunia showed up!

Regina was banned from appearing at the swim meet and was asked to leave the Spirit Squad since her actions showed absolutely no good spirit. Not only had she stolen our mascot, she'd also put the hook in the fishing net at my party, injuring Jada and Kaitlyn. I knew it probably wouldn't be the last we heard from her, but for now no one seemed to care much that she wasn't around.

When it was time for the thirteen-year-old relay race and the horn blew to start, I dove into the water and swam as fast as I could. Shyanna, Rachel, and Cassie all did the same. We came in sixth, and I couldn't have been more proud.

Finally, it was time for my individual race — the butterfly!

All the swimmers took their spots at the starting blocks. My heart pounded as I waited for the buzzer to sound, and when it went off, I swam as fast as I'd ever swum before. I blocked out all the cheers from the crowd, as well as the swimmers in the other lanes, and just focused on doing my best.

When my hand hit the wall on my final lap, I glanced up at the clock. The display board showed that I'd beaten my best time! I'd come in second behind Shelby Stewart, but I knew it wasn't because of the Sea Lion or because of anything else. Shelby had simply swum faster. But I'd done my best, and that's what mattered.

I swam to the stands afterward to sit with my family and help my parents with my sisters. I smiled when I glanced over and saw Shyanna holding the dolphin Kai had made for her. He was on one side of her, and Rachel was on her other side. Shyanna grinned at me and gave me a happy thumbs-up.

I looked around for Jada to see if she was upset after realizing who Kai's crush was, but she was sitting with Finlay from our swim team. She was giggling and seemed oblivious to the fact that Kai was even in the stands. I guess she'd moved on to a new crush.

I smiled and put my attention back on the swimming and cheering for our team. In the end, we won a few races and lost a few, but it was exciting either way. Winning felt better for sure, but so did being a good person instead of a suspicious wreck.

When the races were over, I turned to my mom. My sisters looked exhausted from all the excitement, and I knew they were going to go back to the cave and crash.

"Do you mind if I go to shore to see my friends?" I asked her.

"You mean Justin," Mom teased, making my cheeks burn. That Shyanna! I knew she'd told my mom about my crush on Justin! Mom smiled and then started to giggle when she saw the look on my face. "You can go if Rachel goes with you."

I caught Rachel's eye and made the motion of walking with my fingers. She smiled, understanding that I wanted to go to land and use my legs.

"Look at Shyanna over there with that merboy from Titania," I said to my mom. "He made her that clay dolphin she's holding. You should mention it to her dad. I'm sure he'd be as eager to know about her new friend as you were to learn about Justin." I winked to show I was kidding.

My mom was still laughing when I swam over to Rachel. She grabbed my hand and then rubbed my belly. "For good luck," she said, laughing and taking off through the water.

I chased after her. My friend was much faster than she used to be, but I still caught up to her. A few seconds later, Shyanna joined us, and together, we all headed for shore. Life was good again. I had my best friends. And together, we were unstoppable.

Legend of Mermaids

These creatures of the sea have many secrets. Although people have believed in mermaids for centuries, nobody has ever proven their existence. People all over the world are attracted to the mysterious mermaids.

The earliest mermaid story dates back to around 1000 BC in an Assyrian legend. A goddess loved a human man but killed him accidentally. She fled to the water in shame. She tried to change into a fish, but the water would not let her hide her true nature. She lived the rest of her days as half-woman, half-fish.

Later, the ancient Greeks whispered tales of fishy women called sirens. These beautiful but deadly beings lured sailors to their graves. Many sailors feared or respected mermaids because of their association with doom.

Note: This text was taken from The Girl's Guide to Mermaids: Everything Alluring about These Mythical Beauties *by Sheri A. Johnson (Capstone Press, 2012). For more mermaid facts, be sure to check this book out!*

About the Author

Janet Gurtler has written numerous well-received YA books. Mermiad Kingdom is her debut series for younger readers. She lives in Calgary, Alberta, near the Canadian Rockies, with her husband, son, and a chubby Chihuahua named Bruce. Gurtler does not live in an Igloo or play hockey, but she does love maple syrup and does say "eh" a lot.

About the Illustrator

Katie Wood fell in love with drawing when she was very small. Since graduating from Loughborough University School of Art and Design in 2004, she has been living her dream working as a freelance illustrator. From her studio in Leicester, England, she creates bright and lively illustrations for books and magazines all over the world.

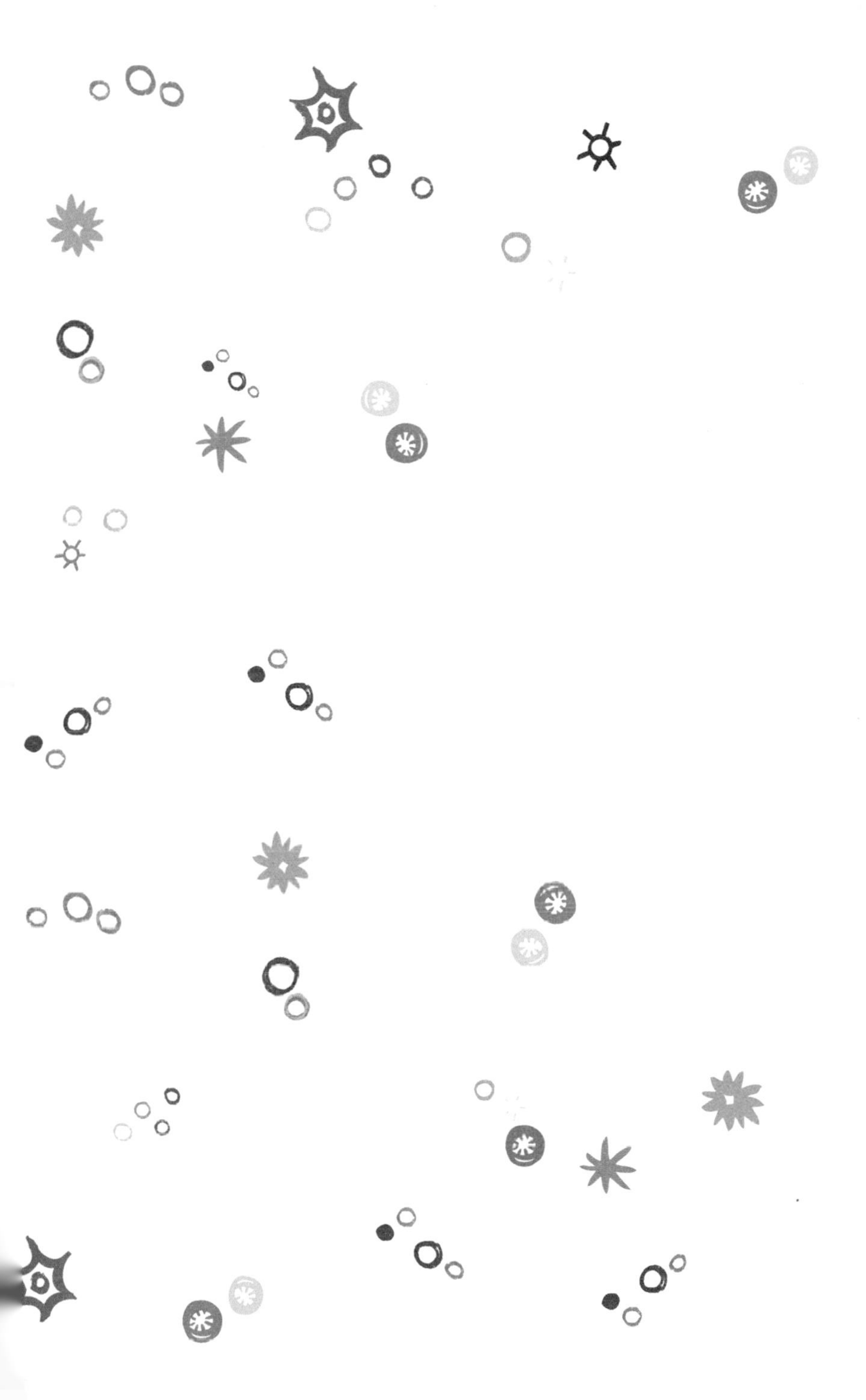